P9-CRO-267

THE
GHOST
FROM
THE
GRAND
BANKS

BOOKS BY ARTHUR C. CLARKE

NON-FICTION

Ascent to Orbit
Astounding Days
The Challenge of the Sea
The Challenge of the Spaceship
The Coast of Coral
The Exploration of the Moon
The Exploration of Space
Going into Space
Interplanetary Flight
The Making of a Moon
Profiles of the Future
The Promise of Space
The Reefs of Taprobane
Report on Planet Three
The View From Serendip
Voice Across the Sea
Voices From the Sky
The Young Traveller in Space
1984: Spring

With the Astronauts
  First on the Moon
With Mike Wilson
  Boy Beneath the Sea
  The First Five Fathoms
  Indian Ocean Adventure
  Indian Ocean Treasure
  The Treasure of the Great Reef
With Peter Hyams
  The Odyssey File
With the Editors of LIFE
  Man and Space

With Robert Silverberg
  Into Space
With Chesley Bonestell
  Beyond Jupiter
With Simon Welfare & John Fairley
  Arthur C. Clarke's
    Mysterious World
  Arthur C. Clarke's
    World of Strange Powers
  Arthur C. Clarke's Chronicles
    of the Strange & Mysterious
*Anthologies

FICTION

*Across the Sea of Stars
Against the Fall of Night
Childhood's End
The City and the Stars
The Deep Range
Dolphin Island
Earthlight
Expedition to Earth
A Fall of Moondust
The Fountains of Paradise
*From the Oceans, From the Stars
Glide Path
Imperial Earth
Islands in the Sky
The Lion of Comarre
The Lost Worlds of 2001
A Meeting With Medusa
*The Nine Billion Names of God
The Other Side of the Sky
*Prelude to Mars
Prelude to Space
Reach for Tomorrow
Rendezvous With Rama
The Sands of Mars
The Songs of Distant Earth
*The Sentinel
*Tales From Planet Earth
Tales From the "White Hart"
Tales of Ten Worlds
The Wind From the Sun
2001: A Space Odyssey
2010: Odyssey Two
2061: Odyssey Three

With Gentry Lee
  Cradle
  Rama II

ARTHUR C. CLARKE HAS EDITED:

The Coming of the Space Age
Arthur C. Clarke's July 20, 2019
Science Fiction Hall of Fame, III
Three for Tomorrow
Time Probe
Arthur C. Clarke's Venus Prime I-VI (Paul Preuss)
Beyond the Fall of Night (Gregory Benford)
Project Solar Sail

ARTHUR C. CLARKE

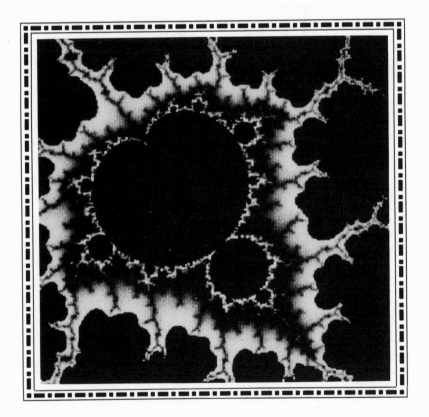

THE

GHOST

FROM

THE

GRAND

BANKS

BANTAM BOOKS
NEW YORK • TORONTO • LONDON • SYDNEY • AUCKLAND

THE GHOST FROM THE GRAND BANKS
A Bantam Book / December 1990

All rights reserved.
Copyright © 1990 by Arthur C. Clarke.
Book design by Barbara Cohen Aronica.
No part of this book may be reproduced or transmitted
in any form or by any means, electronic or mechanical,
including photocopying, recording, or by any information
storage and retrieval system, without permission in writing from
the publisher.
For information address: Bantam Books.

Library of Congress Cataloging-in-Publication Data

Clarke, Arthur Charles, 1917–
    The ghost from the grand banks / by Arthur C. Clarke.
    p.   cm.
    Includes bibliographical references.
ISBN 0-553-07222-6
    I. Title.
    PR6005.L36G48   1990
    823'.914—dc20   90-39698
                                                                  CIP

Published simultaneously in the United States and Canada

Bantam Books are published by Bantam Books, a division of Bantam Doubleday Dell Publishing Group,
Inc. Its trademark, consisting of the words "Bantam Books" and the portrayal of a rooster, is Registered
in U.S. Patent and Trademark Office and in other countries. Marca Registrada. Bantam Books, 666 Fifth
Avenue, New York, New York 10103.

PRINTED IN THE UNITED STATES OF AMERICA

BVG   0 9 8 7 6 5 4 3 2 1

For my old friend Bill MacQuitty—
who, as a boy,
witnessed the launch of R.M.S. Titanic,
and, forty-five years later,
sank her for the second time.

CONTENTS

PRELUDE

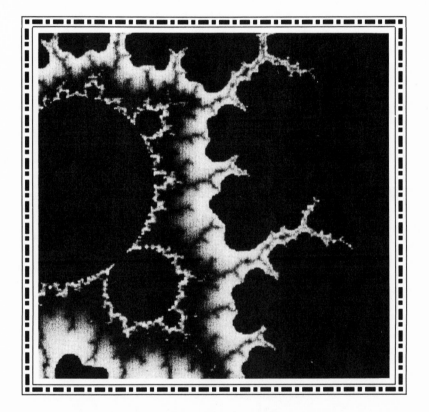

1.
SUMMER
OF '74

THERE MUST BE BETTER WAYS, Jason Bradley kept telling himself, of celebrating one's twenty-first birthday than attending a mass funeral; but at least he had no emotional involvement. He wondered if Operation JENNIFER's director, or his CIA sidekicks, even knew the names of the sixty-three Russian sailors they were now consigning to the deep.

The whole ceremony seemed utterly unreal, and the presence of the camera crew added yet another dimension of fantasy. Jason felt that he was an extra in a Hollywood movie, and that someone would shout "Action!" as the shrouded corpses slid into the sea. After all, it was quite possible—even likely—that Howard Hughes himself had been in the plane that had circled overhead a few hours before. If it was not the Old Man, it must have been some other top brass of the Summa Corporation; no one else knew what was happening in this lonely stretch of the Pacific, a thousand kilometers northwest of Hawaii.

For that matter, not even *Glomar Explorer*'s operations team—carefully insulated from the rest of the ship's crew—

knew anything about the mission until they were already at sea. That they were attempting an unprecedented salvage job was obvious, and the smart money favored a lost reconnaissance satellite. No one dreamed that they were going to lift an entire Russian submarine from water two thousand fathoms deep— with its nuclear warheads, its codebooks, and its cryptographic equipment. And, of course, its crew. . . .

Until this morning—yes, it had been quite a birthday!— Jason had never seen Death. Perhaps it was morbid curiosity that had prompted him to volunteer, when the medics had asked for help to bring the bodies up from the morgue. (The planners in Langley had thought of everything; they had provided refriger- ation for exactly one hundred cadavers.) He had been astonished—and relieved—to find how well preserved most of the corpses were, after six years on the bed of the Pacific. The sailors who had been trapped in sealed compartments, where no predators could reach them, looked as if they were sleeping. Jason felt that, if he had known the Russian for "Wake up!" he would have had an irresistible urge to shout it.

There was certainly someone aboard who knew Russian, and spoke it beautifully, for the entire funeral service had been in that language; only now, at the very end, was English used as *Explorer*'s chaplain came on line with the closing words for burial at sea.

There was a long silence after the last "Amen," followed by a brief command to the Honor Guard. And then, as one by one the lost sailors slid gently over the side, came the music that would haunt Jason Bradley for the rest of his life.

It was sad, yet not like any funeral music that he had ever heard; in its slow, relentless beat was all the power and mystery of the sea. Jason was not a very imaginative young man, but he felt that he was listening to the sound of waves marching forever against some rocky shore. It would be many years before he learned how well this music had been chosen.

The bodies were heavily weighted, so that they entered the water feet first, with only the briefest of splashes. Then they vanished instantly; they would reach their final resting place intact, before the circling sharks could mutilate them.

Jason wondered if the rumor was true, and that in due course the film of this ceremony would be sent to Moscow. It would have been a civilized gesture—but a somewhat ambiguous one. And he doubted that Security would approve, however skillfully the editing was done.

As the last of the sailors returned to the sea, the haunting music ebbed into silence. The sense of doom that had hung over *Explorer* for so many days seemed to disperse, like a fogbank blown away by the wind. There was a long moment of complete silence; then the single word "Dismiss" came from the PA system—not in the usual brusque manner, but so quietly that it was some time before the files of men standing at attention broke up and began to drift away.

And now, thought Jason, I can have a proper birthday party. He never dreamed that one day he would walk this deck again—in another sea, and another century.

2.
THE
COLORS OF
INFINITY

DONALD CRAIG HATED these visits, but he knew that they would continue as long as they both lived; if not through love (had it ever *really* been there?), at least through compassion and a shared grief.

Because it is so hard to see the obvious, it had been months before he realized the true cause of his discomfort. The Torrington Clinic was more like a luxury hotel than a world-famous center for the treatment of psychological disorders. Nobody died here; trolleys never rolled from wards to operating theaters; there were no white-robed doctors making Pavlovian responses to their beepers; and even the attendants never wore uniforms. But it was still, essentially, a *hospital;* and a hospital was where the fifteen-year-old Donald had watched his father gasping for breath, as he slowly died from the first of the two great plagues that had ravaged the Twentieth Century.

"How is she this morning, Dolores?" he asked the nurse after he had checked in at Reception.

"Quite cheerful, Mr. Craig. She asked me to take her shopping—she wants to buy a new hat."

"Shopping! That's the first time she's even asked to go out!"

Donald should have been pleased, yet he felt a twinge of resentment. Edith would never speak to him; indeed, she seemed unaware of his presence, looking through him as if he did not even exist.

"What did Dr. Jafferjee say? Is it okay for her to leave the clinic?"

"I'm afraid not. But it's a good sign: she's starting to show interest in the world around her again."

A new *hat*? thought Craig. That was a typically feminine reaction—but it was not at all typical of Edith. She had always dressed . . . well, sensibly rather than fashionably, and had been quite content to order her clothes in the usual fashion, by teleshopping. Somehow, he could not imagine her in some exclusive Mayfair shop, surrounded by hatboxes, tissue paper, and fawning assistants. But if she felt that way, so be it; anything to help her escape from the mathematical labyrinth which was, quite literally, infinite in extent.

And where was she now, in her endless explorations? As usual, she was sitting crouched in a swivel chair, while an image built up on the meter-wide screen that dominated one wall of her room. Craig could see that it was in hi-res mode—all two thousand lines—so even the supercomputer was going flat out to paint a pixel every few seconds. To a casual observer, it would have seemed that the image was frozen in a partly completed state; only close inspection would have shown that the end of the bottom line was creeping slowly across the screen.

"She started this run," whispered Nurse Dolores, "early

yesterday morning. Of course, she hasn't been sitting here *all* the time. She's sleeping well now, even without sedation."

The image flickered briefly, as one scan line was completed and a new one started creeping from left to right across the screen. More than ninety percent of the picture was now displayed; the lower portion still being generated would show little more of interest.

Despite the dozens—no, hundreds—of times that Donald Craig had watched these images being created, they had never lost their fascination. Part of it came from the knowledge that he was looking at something that no human eye had ever seen before—or ever would see again, if its coordinates were not saved in the computer. Any random search for a lost image would be far more futile than seeking one particular grain of sand in all the deserts of the world.

And where was Edith now, in her endless exploring? He glanced at the small display screen below the main monitor, and checked the magnitude of the enormous numbers that marched across it, digit after implacable digit. They were grouped in fives to make it easier for human eyes to grasp, though there was no way that the human mind could do so.

. . . Six, seven, eight clusters—forty digits all told. That meant—

He did a quick mental calculation—a neglected skill in this day and age, of which he was inordinately proud. The result impressed, but did not surprise him. On this scale, the original basic image would be much bigger than the Galaxy. And the computer could continue expanding it until it was larger than the Cosmos, though at *that* magnification, computing even a single image might take years.

Donald could well understand why Georg Cantor, the discoverer (or was it inventor?) of the numbers beyond infinity, had spent his last years in a mental home. Edith had taken the first steps on that same endless road, aided by machinery beyond the dreams of any Nineteenth-Century mathematician. The computer generating these images was performing trillions of operations a second; in a few hours, it would manipulate more numbers than the entire human race had ever handled, since the first Cro-Magnon started counting pebbles on the floor of his cave.

Though the unfolding patterns never exactly repeated themselves, they fell into a small number of easily recognized categories. There were multipointed stars of six-, eight-fold, and even higher degrees of symmetry; spirals that sometimes resembled the trunks of elephants, and at other times the tentacles of octopods; black amoebae linked by networks of contorted tendrils; faceted, compound insect eyes. . . . Because there was absolutely no sense of scale, some of the figures being created on the screen could have been equally well interpreted as bizarre galaxies—or the microfauna in a drop of ditchwater.

And ever and again, as the computer increased the degree of magnification and dived deeper into the geometric depths it was exploring, the original strange shape—looking like a fuzzy figure eight lying on its side—that contained all this controlled chaos would reappear. Then the endless cycle would begin again, though with variations so subtle that they eluded the eye.

Surely, thought Donald, Edith must realize, in some part of her mind, that she is trapped in an endless loop. What had happened to the wonderful brain that had conceived and designed the '99 Phage which, in the early hours of 1 January 2000, had briefly made her one of the most famous women in the world?

"Edith," he said softly, "this is Donald. Is there anything I can do?"

Nurse Dolores was looking at him with an unfathomable expression. She had never been actually unfriendly, but her greetings always lacked warmth. Sometimes he wondered if she blamed him for Edith's condition.

That was a question he had asked himself every day, in the months since the tragedy.

3.

A BETTER
MOUSETRAP

ROY EMERSON CONSIDERED HIMSELF, accurately enough, to be reasonably good-natured, but there was one thing that could make him *really* angry. It had happened on what he swore would be his last TV appearance, when the interviewer on a Late, Late Show had asked, with malice aforethought: "Surely, the principle of the Wave Wiper is very straightforward. Why didn't someone invent it earlier?" The host's tone of voice made his real meaning perfectly clear: "Of course *I* could have thought of it myself, if I hadn't more important things to do."

Emerson resisted the temptation of replying: "If you had the chance, I'm sure you'd ask Einstein, or Edison, or Newton, the same sort of question." Instead, he answered mildly enough: "Well, *someone* had to be the first. I guess I was the lucky one."

"What gave you the idea? Did you suddenly jump out of the bathtub shouting 'Eureka'?"

Had it not been for the host's cynical attitude, the question would have been fairly innocuous. Of course, Emerson had heard it a hundred times before. He switched to automatic mode and mentally pressed the PLAY button.

"What gave me the idea—though I didn't realize it at the time—was a ride in a high-speed Coast Guard patrol boat off Key West, back in '03 . . ."

Though it had led him to fame and fortune, even now Emerson preferred not to recall certain aspects of that trip. It had seemed a good idea at the time—a short pleasure cruise through Hemingway's old stomping grounds, at the invitation of a cousin in the Coast Guard. How amazed Ernest would have been at the target of their antismuggling activities—blocks of crystal, about the size of a matchbox, that had made their way from Hong Kong via Cuba. But these TIMs—Terabyte Interactive Microlibraries—had put so many U.S. publishers out of business that Congress had dusted off legislation that dated back to the heydays of Prohibition.

Yes, it had sounded very attractive—while he was still on terra firma. What Emerson had forgotten (or his cousin had neglected to tell him) was that smugglers preferred to operate in the worst weather they could find, short of a Gulf hurricane.

"It was a rough trip, and about the only thing I remembered afterwards was the gadget on the bridge that allowed the helmsman to see ahead, despite the torrents of rain and spray that were being dumped on us.

"It was simply a disc of glass, spinning at high speed. No water could stay on it for more than a fraction of a second, so it was always perfectly transparent. I thought at the time it was far better than a car's windshield wiper; and then I forgot all about it."

"For how long?"

"I'm ashamed to say. Oh, maybe a couple of years. Then one day I was driving through a heavy rainstorm in the New Jersey countryside, and my wipers jammed; I had to pull off the road until the storm had passed. I was stuck for maybe half an hour; and at the end of that time, the whole thing was clear in my mind."

"*That's* all it took?"

"Plus every cent I could lay my hands on, and two years of fifteen-hour days and seven-day weeks in my garage." (Emerson might have added "And my marriage," but he suspected that his host already knew that. He was famed for his careful research.)

"Spinning the windshield—or even part of it—obviously wasn't practical. *Vibrations* had to be the answer; but what kind?

"First I tried to drive the whole windshield like a loudspeaker cone. That certainly kept the rain off, but then there was the noise problem. So I went ultrasonic; it took kilowatts of power—and all the dogs in the neighborhood went crazy. Worse still, few windshields lasted more than a couple of hours before they turned into powdered glass.

"So I tried *sub*sonics. They worked better—but gave you a bad headache after a few minutes of driving. Even if you couldn't hear them, you could feel them.

"I was stuck for months, and almost gave up the whole idea, when I realized my mistake. I was trying to vibrate the whole massive sheet of multiplex safety glass—sometimes as much as ten kilograms of it. All I needed to keep dancing was a thin layer on the outside; even if it was only a few microns thick, it would keep the rainwater off.

"So I read all I could about surface waves, transducers, impedance matching—"

"Whoa! Can we have that in words of one syllable?"

"Frankly, no. All I can say is that I found a way of confining low-energy vibrations to a very thin surface layer, leaving the main bulk of the windshield unaffected. If you want details, I refer you to the basic patents."

"Happy to take your word for it, Mr. Emerson. Now, our next guest—"

Possibly because the interview had taken place in London, where the works of the New England transcendentalist were not everyday reading, Emerson's host had failed to make the connection with his famous namesake (no relation, as far as he knew). No American interviewer, of course, missed the opportunity of complimenting Roy on inventing the apocryphal Better Mousetrap. The automobile industry had indeed beaten a path to his door; within a few years, almost all the world's millions of metronoming blades had been replaced by the Sonic Wave Windshield Wiper. Even more important, thousands of accidents had been averted, with the improvement of visibility in bad-weather driving.

It was while testing the latest model of his invention that Roy Emerson made his next breakthrough—and, once again, he was very lucky that no one else had thought of it first.

His '04 Mercedes Hydro was cruising in benign silence down Park Avenue, living up to its celebrated slogan "You can drink your exhaust!" Midtown seemed to have been hit by a monsoon: conditions were perfect for testing the Mark V Wave Wiper. Emerson was sitting beside his chauffeur—he no longer drove himself, of course—quietly dictating notes as he adjusted the electronics.

The car seemed to be sliding between the rain-washed walls of a glass canyon. Emerson had driven this way a hundred times before, but only now did the blindingly obvious hit him with paralyzing force.

Then he recovered his breath, and said to the carcom: "Get me Joe Wickram."

His lawyer, sunning himself on a yacht off the Great Barrier Reef, was a little surprised by the call.

"This is going to cost you, Roy. I was just about to gaff a marlin."

Emerson was in no mood for such trivialities.

"Tell me, Joe—does the patent cover *all* applications—not just car windshields?"

Joe was hurt at the implied criticism.

"Of course. That's why I put in the clause about adaptive circuits, so it could automatically adjust to any shape and size. Thinking of a new line in sunglasses?"

"Why not? But I've got something slightly bigger in mind. Remember that the Wave Wiper doesn't merely keep off water— it shakes off *any* dirt that's already there. Do you remember when you last saw a car with a really dirty windshield?"

"Not now you mention it."

"Thanks. That's all I wanted to know. Good luck with the fishing."

Roy Emerson leaned back in his seat and did some mental calculation. He wondered if all the windshields of all the cars in the city of New York could match the area of glass in the single building he was now driving past.

He was about to destroy an entire profession; armies of window cleaners would soon be looking for other jobs.

Until now, Roy Emerson had been merely a millionaire. Soon he would be rich.

And bored. . . .

4.

THE
CENTURY
SYNDROME

WHEN THE CLOCKS STRUCK midnight on Friday, 31 December 1999, there could have been few educated people who did not realize that the Twenty-first Century would not begin for another year. For weeks, all the media had been explaining that because the Western calendar started with Year 1, not Year 0, the Twentieth Century still had twelve months to go.

It made no difference; the psychological effect of those three zeros was too powerful, the fin de siècle ambience too overwhelming. *This* was the weekend that counted; 1 January 2001 would be an anticlimax, except to a few movie buffs.

There was also a very practical reason why 1 January 2000 was the date that really mattered, and it was a reason that would never have occurred to anyone a mere forty years earlier. Since the 1960s, more and more of the world's accounting had been taken over by computers, and the process was now essentially complete. Millions of optical and electronic memories held in their stores trillions of transactions—virtually all the business of the planet.

And, of course, most of these entries bore a date. As the last decade of the century opened, something like a shock wave passed through the financial world. It was suddenly, and belatedly, realized that most of those dates lacked a vital component.

The *human* bank clerks and accountants who did what was still called "bookkeeping" had very seldom bothered to write in the "19" before the two digits they had entered. These were taken for granted; it was a matter of common sense. And common sense, unfortunately, was what computers so conspicuously lacked. Come the first dawn of '00, myriads of electronic morons would say to themselves "00 is smaller than 99. Therefore today is earlier than yesterday—by exactly 99 years. Recalculate all mortgages, overdrafts, interest-bearing accounts on this basis. . . ." The results would be international chaos on a scale never witnessed before; it would eclipse all earlier achievements of artificial stupidity—even Black Monday, 5 June 1995, when a faulty chip in Zurich had set the bank rate at 150 percent instead of 15 percent.

There were not enough programmers in the world to check all the billions of financial statements that existed, and to add the magic "19" prefix wherever necessary. The only solution was to design special software that could perform the task, by being injected—like a benign virus—into all the programs involved.

During the closing years of the century, most of the world's star-class programmers were engaged in the race to develop a "Vaccine '99"; it had become a kind of Holy Grail. Several faulty versions were issued as early as 1997—and wiped out any purchasers who hastened to test them before making adequate backups. The lawyers did very well out of the ensuing suits and countersuits.

Edith Craig belonged to the small pantheon of famous women programmers that began with Byron's tragic daughter Ada, Lady Lovelace, continued through Rear Admiral Grace Hopper, and culminated with Dr. Susan Calvin. With the help of only a dozen assistants and one SuperCray, she had designed the quarter million lines of code of the DOUBLEZERO program that would prepare any well-organized financial system to face the Twenty-first Century. It could even deal with *badly* organized ones, inserting the computer equivalent of red flags at danger points where human intervention might still be necessary.

It was just as well that 1 January 2000 was a Saturday; most of the world had a full weekend to recover from its hangover—and to prepare for the moment of truth on Monday morning.

The following week saw a record number of bankruptcies among firms whose accounts receivable had been turned into instant garbage. Those who had been wise enough to invest in DOUBLEZERO survived, and Edith Craig was rich, famous . . . and happy.

Only the wealth and the fame would last.

5.
EMPIRE OF GLASS

ROY EMERSON HAD NEVER EXPECTED to be rich, so he was not adequately prepared for the ordeal. At first he had naively imagined that he could hire experts to look after his rapidly accumulating wealth, leaving him to do exactly what he pleased with his time. He had soon discovered that this was only partly true: money could provide freedom, but it also brought responsibility. There were countless decisions that he alone could make, and a depressing number of hours had to be spent with lawyers and accountants.

Halfway to his first billion, he found himself chairman of the board. The company had only five directors—his mother, his older brother, his younger sister, Joe Wickram, and himself.

"Why not Diana?" he had asked Joe.

Emerson's attorney looked at him over the spectacles which, he fondly believed, gave him an air of distinction in this age of ten-minute corrective eye surgery.

"Parents and siblings are forever," he said. "Wives come

and go—*you* should know that. Not, of course, that I'm suggesting . . ."

Joe was right; Diana had indeed gone, like Gladys before her. It had been a fairly amicable, though expensive, departure, and when the last documents had been signed, Emerson disappeared into his workshop for several months. When he emerged (without any new inventions, because he had been too engrossed in discovering how to operate his wonderful new equipment to actually *use* it) Joe was waiting for him with a new surprise.

"It won't take much of your time," he said, "and it's a great honor: Parkinson's are one of the most distinguished firms in England, established over two hundred years ago. And it's the first time they've *ever* taken a director from outside the family—let alone a foreigner."

"Ha! I suppose they need more capital."

"Of course. But it's to your mutual interest—and they really respect you. You know what you've done to the glass business, worldwide."

"Will I have to wear a top hat and—what do they call them—spats?"

"Only if you want to be presented at court, which *they* could easily arrange."

To his considerable surprise, Roy Emerson had found the experience not only enjoyable, but stimulating. Until he joined the board of Parkinson's and attended its bimonthly meetings in the City of London, he thought he knew something about glass. He very quickly discovered his mistake.

Even ordinary plate glass, which he had taken for granted all his life—and which contributed to most of his fortune—had a history which astonished him. Emerson had never asked himself how it was made, assuming that it was squeezed out of the molten raw material between giant rollers.

So indeed it had been, until the middle of the twentieth century—and the resulting rough sheets had required hours of expensive polishing. Then a crazy Englishman had said: Why not let gravity and surface tension do all the work? Let the glass *float* on a river of molten metal: that will automatically give a perfectly smooth surface. . . .

After a few years, and a few million pounds, his colleagues suddenly stopped laughing. Overnight, "float glass" made all other methods of manufacturing obsolete.

Emerson was much impressed by this piece of technological history, recognizing its parallel with his own breakthrough. And he was honest enough to admit that it had required far more courage and commitment than his own modest invention. It exemplified the difference between genius and talent.

He was also fascinated by the ancient art of the glassblower, who had *not* been wholly replaced by technology and probably never would be. He even paid a visit to Venice, now cowering nervously behind its Dutch-built dikes, and goggled at the intricate marvels in the Glass Museum. Not only was it impossible to imagine how some of them had been manufactured, it was incredible that they had even been *moved* intact from their place of origin. There seemed no limit to the things that could be done with glass, and new uses were still being discovered after two thousand years.

On one particularly dull board meeting Emerson had been frankly daydreaming, admiring the nearby dome of St. Paul's from one of the few vantage points that had survived commercial greed and architectural vandalism. Two more items on the agenda and they'd be at Any Other Business; then they could all go to the excellent lunch that was waiting in the Penthouse Suite.

The words "four hundred atmospheres pressure" made him look up. Sir Roger Parkinson was reading from a letter which he was holding as if it were some species of hitherto unknown insect. Emerson quickly riffled through the thick folder of his agenda and found his own copy.

It was on impressive stationery, but the usual polynomial legal name meant nothing to him; he noted approvingly, however, that the address was in Lincoln's Inn Fields. At the bottom of the sheet, like a modest cough, were the words "Est. 1803," in letters barely visible to the naked eye.

"They don't give the name of their client," said young (thirty-five if he was a day) George Parkinson. "Interesting."

"Whoever he is," interjected William Parkinson-Smith— the family's secretly admired black sheep, much beloved by the gossip channels for his frequent domestic upheavals—"he doesn't seem to know what he wants. Why should he ask for quotes on such a range of sizes? From a millimeter, for heaven's sake, up to a half-meter radius."

"The larger size," said Rupert Parkinson, famous racing yachtsman, "reminds me of those Japanese fishing floats that get washed up all over the Pacific. Make splendid ornaments."

"I can think of only one use for the smallest size," said George portentously. "Fusion power."

"Nonsense, Uncle," interjected Gloria Windsor-Parkinson (100 Meters Silver, 2004 Olympics). "Laser-zapping was given up years ago—and the microspheres for that were *tiny*. Even a millimeter would be far too big—unless you wanted a house-broken H-bomb."

"Besides, look at the quantities required," said Arnold Parkinson (world authority on Pre-Raphaelite art). "Enough to fill the Albert Hall."

"Wasn't that the title of a Beatles song?" asked William. There was a thoughtful silence, then a quick scrabbling at keyboards. Gloria, as usual, got there first.

"Nice try, Uncle Bill. It's from *Sergeant Pepper*—'A Day in the Life.' I had no idea you were fond of classical music."

Sir Roger let the free-association process go its way unchecked. He could bring the board to an instant full stop by lifting an eyebrow, but he was too wise to do so—yet. He knew how often these brainstorming sessions led to vital conclusions—even decisions—that mere logic would never have discovered. And even when they fizzled out, they helped the members of his worldwide family to know each other better.

But it was Roy Emerson (token Yank) who was to amaze the massed Parkinsons with his inspired guess. For the last few minutes, an idea had been forming in the back of his mind. Rupert's reference to the Japanese fishing floats had provided the first vague hint, but it would never have come to anything without one of those extraordinary coincidences that no self-respecting novelist would allow in a work of fiction.

Emerson was sitting almost facing the portrait of Basil Parkinson, 1874–1912. And everyone knew where *he* had died, though the exact circumstances were still the stuff of legend—and at least one libel action.

There were some who said that he had tried to disguise himself as a woman, so that he could get into one of the last boats to leave. Others had seen him in animated conversation with Chief Designer Andrews, completely ignoring the icy water rising around his ankles. This version was considered—at least by the family—to be far more probable. The two brilliant engineers would have enjoyed each other's company, during the last minutes of their lives.

Emerson cleared his throat, a little nervously. He might be making a fool of himself . . .

"Sir Roger," he said. "I've just had a crazy idea. You've all seen the publicity and speculations about the centennial, now that it's only five years to 2012. A few million bubbles of toughened glass would be just right for the job everyone's talking about.

"*I* think our mystery customer is after the *Titanic*."

6.
"A NIGHT
TO
REMEMBER"

ALTHOUGH MOST OF THE HUMAN RACE had seen his handiwork, Donald Craig would never be as famous as his wife. Yet his programming skills had made him equally rich, and their meeting was inevitable, for they had both used supercomputers to solve a problem unique to the last decade of the Twentieth Century.

In the mid-90s, the movie and TV studios had suddenly realized that they were facing a crisis that no one had ever anticipated, although it should have been obvious years in advance. Many of the classics of the cinema—the capital assets of the enormous entertainment industry—were becoming worthless, because fewer and fewer people could bear to watch them. Millions of viewers would switch off in disgust at a western, a James Bond thriller, a Neil Simon comedy, a courtroom drama, for a reason which would have been inconceivable only a generation before. *They showed people smoking.*

The AIDS epidemic of the '90s had been partly responsible for this revolution in human behavior. The Twentieth Century's Second Plague was appalling enough, but it killed only a few percent of those who died, equally horribly, from the innumerable diseases triggered by tobacco. Donald's father had been among them, and there was poetic justice in the fact that his son had made several fortunes by "sanitizing" classic movies so that they could be presented to the new public.

Though some were so wreathed in smoke that they were beyond redemption, in a surprising number of cases skillful computer processing could remove offending cylinders from actors' hands or mouths, and banish ashtrays from tabletops. The techniques that had seamlessly welded real and imaginary worlds in such landmark movies as *Who Framed Roger Rabbit?* had countless other applications—not all of them legal. However, unlike the video blackmailers, Donald Craig could claim to be performing a useful social function.

He had met Edith at a screening of his sanitized *Casablanca,* and she had at once pointed out how it could have been improved. Although the trade joked that he had married Edith for her algorithms, the match had been a success on both the personal and professional levels. For the first few years, at least . . .

". . . This will be a very simple job," said Edith Craig when the last credits rolled off the monitor. "There are only four scenes in the whole movie that present problems. And what a joy to work in good old black and white!"

Donald was still silent. The film had shaken him more than he cared to admit, and his cheeks were still moist with tears. What is it, he asked himself, that moves me so much? The fact that this *really* happened, and that the names of all the hundreds of people he had seen die—even if in a studio reenactment—

were still on record? No, it had to be something more than that, because he was not the sort of man who cried easily. . . .

Edith hadn't noticed. She had called up the first logged sequence on the monitor screen, and was looking thoughtfully at the frozen image.

"Starting with Frame 3751," she said. "Here we go—man lighting cigar—man on right screen ditto—end on Frame 4432—whole sequence forty-five seconds—what's the client's policy on cigars?"

"Okay in case of historical necessity; remember the Churchill retrospective? No way we could pretend *he* didn't smoke."

Edith gave that short laugh, rather like a bark, that Donald now found more and more annoying.

"I've never been able to imagine Winston without a cigar—and I must say he seemed to thrive on them. After all, he lived to ninety."

"He was lucky; look at poor Freud—years of agony before he asked his doctor to kill him. And toward the end, the wound stank so much that even his dog wouldn't go near him."

"Then you don't think a group of 1912 millionaires qualifies under 'historical necessity'?"

"Not unless it affects the story line—and it doesn't. So I vote clean it up."

"Very well—Algorithm Six will do it, with a few subroutines."

Edith's fingers danced briefly over the keyboard as she entered the command. She had learned never to challenge her partner's decisions in these matters; he was still too emotionally involved, though it was now almost twenty years since he had watched his father struggling for one more breath.

"Frame 6093," said Edith. "Cardsharp fleecing his wealthy

victims. Some on the left have cigars, but I don't think many people would notice."

"Agreed," Donald answered, somewhat reluctantly. "If we can cut out that cloud of smoke on the right. Try one pass with the haze algorithm."

It was strange, he thought, how one thing could lead to another, and another, and another—and finally to a goal which seemed to have no possible connection with the starting point. The apparently intractable problem of eliminating smoke, and restoring hidden pixels in partially obliterated images, had led Edith into the world of Chaos Theory, of discontinuous functions, and trans-Euclidean meta-geometries.

From that she had swiftly moved into fractals, which had dominated the mathematics of the Twentieth Century's last decade. Donald had begun to worry about the time she now spent exploring weird and wonderful imaginary landscapes, of no practical value—in *his* opinion—to anyone.

"Right," Edith continued. "We'll see how Subroutine 55 handles it. Now Frame 9873—just after they've hit. . . . This man's playing with the pieces of ice on deck—but note those spectators at the left."

"Not worth bothering about. Next."

"Frame 21,397. No way we can save this sequence! Not only *cigarettes*, but those page boys smoking them can't be more than sixteen or seventeen. Luckily, the scene isn't important."

"Well, that's easy; we'll just cut it out. Anything else?"

"No—except for the sound track at Frame 52,763—in the lifeboat. Irate lady exclaims: 'That man over there—he's smoking a cigarette! I think it's disgraceful, at a time like this!' We don't actually *see* him, though."

Donald laughed.

"Nice touch—especially in the circumstances. Leave it in."

"Agreed. But you realize what this means? The whole job

will only take a couple of days—we've already made the analog-digital transfer."

"Yes—we mustn't make it seem too easy! When does the client want it?"

"For once, not last week. After all, it's still only 2007. Five years to go before the centennial."

"That's what puzzles me," said Donald thoughtfully. "Why so early?"

"Haven't you been watching the news, Donald? No one's come out into the open yet, but people are making long-range plans—and trying to raise money. And they've got to do a lot of *that*—before they can bring up the *Titanic*."

"I've never taken those reports seriously. After all, she's badly smashed up—and in two pieces."

"They say that will make it easier. And you can solve any engineering problem—if you throw enough cash at it."

Donald was silent. He had scarcely heard Edith's words, for one of the scenes he had just watched had suddenly replayed itself in his memory. It was as if he was watching it again on the screen; and now he knew why he had wept in the darkness.

"Goodbye, my dear son," the aristocratic young Englishman had said, as the sleeping boy who would never see his father again was passed into the lifeboat.

And yet, before he had died in the icy Atlantic waters, that man had known and loved a son—and Donald Craig envied him. Even before they had started to drift apart, Edith had been implacable. She had given him a daughter; but Ada Craig would never have a brother.

7.

THIRD
LEADER

FROM THE LONDON *Times* (Hardcopy and NewsSat) 2007
April 15:

A Night to Forget?

Some artifacts have the power to drive men mad.
Perhaps the most famous examples are Stonehenge, the
Pyramids, and the hideous statues of Easter Island.
Crackpot theories—even quasi-religious cults—have
flourished around all three.

Now we have another example of this curious
obsession with some relic of the past. In five years'
time, it will be exactly a century since the most famous
of all maritime disasters, the sinking of the luxury liner
Titanic on her maiden voyage in 1912. The tragedy
inspired dozens of books and at least five films—as
well as Thomas Hardy's embarrassingly feeble poem,
"The Convergence of the Twain."

For seventy-three years the great ship lay on the bed of the Atlantic, a monument to the 1,500 souls who were lost with her; she seemed forever beyond human ken. But in 1985, thanks to revolutionary advances in submarine technology, she was discovered, and hundreds of her pitiful relics brought back to the light of day. Even at the time, many considered this a kind of desecration.

Now, according to rumour, much more ambitious plans are afoot; various consortia—as yet unidentified—have been formed to raise the ship, despite her badly damaged condition.

Frankly, such a project seems completely absurd, and we trust that none of our readers will be induced to invest in it. Even if all the engineering problems can be overcome, just what would the salvors *do* with forty or fifty thousand tons of scrap iron? Marine archaeologists have known for years that metal objects—except, of course, gold—disintegrate rapidly when brought into contact with air after long submergence.

Protecting the *Titanic* might be even more expensive than salvaging her. It is not as if—like the *Vasa* or the *Mary Rose*—she is a "time capsule" giving us a glimpse of a lost era. The twentieth century is adequately—sometimes all *too* adequately—documented. We can learn nothing that we do not already know from the debris four kilometres down off the Grand Banks of Newfoundland.

There is no need to revisit her to be reminded of the most important lesson the *Titanic* can teach—the dangers of over-confidence, of technological hubris.

Chernobyl, *Challenger*, *Lagrange* 3 and Experimental Fusor One have shown us where *that* can lead.

Of course we should not forget the *Titanic*. But we should let her rest in peace.

8.
PRIVATE
VENTURE

ROY EMERSON WAS BORED, as usual—though this was a fact that he hated to admit, even to himself. There were times when he would wander through his superbly equipped workshop, with its gleaming machine tools and tangles of electronic gear, quite unable to decide which of his expensive toys he wished to play with next. Sometimes he would start on a project suggested by one of the countless network "magazines," and join a group of similarly inclined hobbyists scattered all over the world. He seldom knew their names—only their often facetious call signs—and he was careful not to give his. Since he had been listed as one of the hundred richest men in the United States, he had learned the value of anonymity.

After a few weeks, however, the latest project would lose its novelty, and he would pull the plug on his unseen playmates, changing his ident code so that they could no longer contact him. For a few days, he would drink too much, and waste time exploring the personal notice boards whose contents would have appalled the first pioneers of electronic communication.

Occasionally—after the long-suffering Joe Wickram had checked it out—he would answer some advertisement for "personal services" that intrigued him. The results were seldom very satisfying, and did nothing to improve his self-respect. The news that Diana had just remarried hardly surprised him, but left him depressed for several days, even though he tried to embarrass her by a vulgarly expensive wedding present.

All play and no work was making Emerson a very dull Roy. Then, overnight, a call from Rupert Parkinson, aboard his racing trimaran in the South Pacific, abruptly changed his life.

"What's your phone cipher?" was Rupert's unexpected opening remark.

"Why . . . normally I don't bother. But I can switch to NSA 2 if it's really important. Only problem, it tends to chop speech on long-distance circuits. So don't talk too fast, and don't overdo that Oxford accent."

"Cambridge, please—*and* Harvard. Here we go."

There was a five-second pause, filled with strange beepings and twitterings. Then Rupert Parkinson, still recognizable though subtly distorted, was back on the line.

"Can you hear me? Fine. Now, you remember that last board meeting, and the item about the glass microspheres?"

"Of course," Emerson answered, a little nervously; he wondered again if he had made a fool of himself. "You were going to look into it. Was my guess correct?"

"Bang on, old man—to coin an expression. Our lawyers had some expensive lunches with *their* lawyers, and we did a few sums together. They never told us who the client was, but we found out easily enough. A British video network—doesn't matter which—thought it would make a splendid series—in real time, culminating with the actual raising. But they lost interest when they found what it would cost, and the deal's off."

"Pity. What *would* it cost?"

"Just to manufacture enough spheres to lift fifty kilotons, at least twenty million dollars. But that would be merely the beginning. You've got to get them down there, properly distributed. You can't just squirt them into the hull; even if they'd stay put, they'd soon tear the ship apart. And I'm only talking about the forward section, of course—the smashed-up stern's another problem.

"Then you've got to get it unstuck from the seabed—it's half buried in mud. That will mean a lot of work by submersibles, and there aren't many that can operate four klicks down. I don't think you could do the job for less than a hundred million. It might even be several times as much."

"So the deal's off. Then why are you calling me?"

"Never thought you'd ask. I've been doing a little private venturing of my own; after all, we Parkinsons have a vested interest. Great-Granddad's down there—or at least his baggage, in suite three, starboard."

"A hundred megabucks worth?"

"Quite possibly—but that's unimportant; some things are beyond price. Have you ever heard of Andrea Bellini?"

"Sounds like a baseball player."

"He was the greatest craftsman in glass that Venice ever produced. To this day, we don't know how he made some of his— Anyway, back in the eighteen seventies we managed to buy the cream of the Glass Museum's collection; in its way it was as big a prize as the Elgin Marbles. For years, the Smithsonian had been begging us to arrange a loan, but we always refused—too risky to send such a priceless cargo across the Atlantic. Until, of course, someone built an unsinkable ship. *Then* we had no excuse."

"Fascinating—and now you've mentioned him, I remember seeing some of Bellini's work the last time I was in Venice. But wouldn't it all be smashed to pieces?"

"Almost certainly not: it was expertly packed, as you can imagine. And anyway, masses of the ship's crockery survived, even though it was completely unprotected. Remember that White Star dining set they auctioned at Sotheby's a couple of years ago?"

"Okay—I'll grant you that. But it seems a little extravagant to raise the whole ship, just for a few crates."

"Of course it is. But it's one major reason why we Parkinsons should get involved."

"And the others?"

"You've been on the board long enough to know that a little publicity doesn't do any harm. The whole world would know *whose* product did the lifting."

Still not good enough, Emerson said to himself. Parkinson's was doing very nicely—and by no means all of the publicity would be favorable. To many people, the wreck was almost sacred; they branded those who tampered with it as grave-robbers.

But he knew that men often concealed—even failed to recognize—their true motives. Since he had joined the board, he had grown to know and like Rupert, though he would hardly call him a close friend; it was not easy for an outsider to get close to the Parkinsons.

Rupert had his own account to settle with the sea. Five years ago, it had taken his beautiful twenty-five-meter yacht *Aurora,* when she had been dismasted by a freak squall off the Scillies, and smashed to pieces on the cruel rocks that had claimed so many victims through the centuries. By pure chance, he had not been aboard; it had been a routine trip—a "bus run"—from Cowes to Bristol for a refit. All the crew had been lost—including the skipper. Rupert Parkinson had never quite recovered; at the same time he had lost both his ship and, as was well known, his lover. The playboy image he now wore in self-defense was only skin deep.

"All very interesting, Rupert. But exactly what do you have in mind? Surely you don't expect *me* to get involved!"

"Yes and no. At the moment, it's a—what do they call it?—*thought experiment.* I'd like to get a feasibility study done, and I'm prepared to finance that myself. Then, if the project makes any sense at all, I'll present it to the board."

"But a *hundred million*! There's no way the company would risk that much. The shareholders would have us behind bars in no time. Whether in a jail or a lunatic asylum, I'm not sure."

"It might cost more—but I'm not expecting Parkinson's to put up all the capital. Maybe twenty or thirty M. I have some friends who'll be able to match that."

"Still not enough."

"Exactly."

There was a long silence, broken only by faintly querulous bleeps from the real-time decoding system as it searched in vain for something to unscramble.

"Very well," said Emerson at last. "I'll go fifty-fifty with you—on the feasibility report, at any rate. Who's your expert? Will I know him?"

"I think so. Jason Bradley."

"Oh—the giant octopus man."

"That was just a sideshow. But look what it did to *his* public image."

"And his fee, I'm sure. Have you sounded him out? Is he interested?"

"Very—but then, so is every ocean engineering firm in the business. I'm sure some of them will be prepared to put up their own money—or at least work on a no-profit basis, just for the P.R."

"Okay—go ahead. But frankly, I think it's a waste of money; we'll just end up with some very expensive reading matter, when Mr. Bradley delivers his report. Anyway, I don't see what you'll do with fifty thousand tons, or whatever it is, of rusty scrap iron."

"Leave that to me—I've a few more ideas, but I don't want to talk about them yet. If some of them work out, the project would pay for itself—eventually. You might even make a profit."

Emerson doubted if that "you" was a slip of the tongue. Rupert was a very smooth operator, and knew exactly what he was doing. And he certainly knew that his listener could easily underwrite the whole operation—if he wished.

"Just one other thing," Parkinson continued. "Until I give the okay—which won't be until I get Bradley's report—not a word to anyone. *Especially* Sir Roger—he'll think we're crazy."

"You mean to say," Emerson retorted, "that there could be the slightest possible doubt?"

9.

PROPHETS
WITH SOME
HONOR

To: The Editor, The London *Times*
From: Lord Aldiss of Brightfount, O.M.
      President Emeritus, Science Fiction World As-
      sociation

Dear Sir,

Your Third Leader (07 Apr 15) concerning plans to raise the *Titanic* again demonstrates what an impact this disaster—by no means the worst in maritime history—has had upon the imagination of mankind.

One extraordinary aspect of the tragedy is that it had been described, with uncanny precision, *fourteen years in advance*. According to Walter Lord's classic account of the disaster, *A Night to Remember*, in 1898 a "struggling author named Morgan Robertson concocted a novel about a fabulous Atlantic liner, far larger than any that had ever been built. Robertson loaded it with rich and complacent people, and then wrecked it one cold April night on an iceberg."

The fictional liner had almost exactly the *Titanic's* size, speed, and displacement. It also carried 3,000 people, and lifeboats for only a fraction of them. . . .

Coincidence, of course. But there is one little detail that chills my blood. Robertson called his ship the *Titan*.

I would also like to draw attention to the fact that two members of the profession I am honoured to represent—that of writers of science fiction—went down with the *Titanic*. One, Jacques Futrelle, is now almost forgotten, and even his nationality is uncertain. But he had attained sufficient success at the age of thirty-seven with *The Diamond Master* and *The Thinking Machine* to travel first class with his wife (who, like 97% of first-class ladies, and only 55% of third-class ones, survived the sinking).

Far more famous was a man who wrote only one book, *A Journey in Other Worlds: A Romance of the Future,* which was published in 1894. This somewhat mystical tour around the Solar System, in the year 2000, described anti-gravity and other marvels. Arkham House reprinted the book on its centennial.

I described the author as "famous," but that is a gross understatement. His name is the *only* one that appears above the huge headline of the *New York American* for 16 April 1912: "1,500 TO 1,800 DEAD."

He was the multi-millionaire John Jacob Astor, sometimes labelled as "the richest man in the world."

He was certainly the richest writer of science fiction who ever lived—a fact which may well mortify admirers of the late L. Ron Hubbard, should any still exist.

I have the honor to be, Sir,
Yours sincerely,
Aldiss of Brightfount, O.M.
President Emeritus, SFWA

10.
"THE ISLE
OF THE
DEAD"

EVERY TRADE HAS its acknowledged leaders, whose fame seldom extends beyond the boundaries of their profession. At any given time, few could name the world's top accountant, dentist, sanitary engineer, insurance broker, mortician . . . to mention only a handful of unglamorous but essential occupations.

There are some ways of making a living, however, which have such high visibility that their practitioners become household names. First, of course, are the performing arts, in which anyone who becomes a star may be instantly recognizable to a large fraction of the human race. Sports and politics are close behind; and so, a cynic might argue, is crime.

Jason Bradley fit into none of these categories, and had never expected to be famous. The *Glomar Explorer* episode was more than three decades in the past, and even if it had not been shrouded in secrecy, his role had been far too obscure to be noteworthy. Although he had been approached several times by writers hoping to get a new angle on Operation JENNIFER, nothing had ever come of their efforts.

It seemed likely that, even at this date, the CIA felt that the single book on the subject was one too many, and had taken steps to discourage other authors. For several years after 1974, Bradley had been visited by anonymous but polite gentlemen who had reminded him of the documents he signed when he was discharged. They always came in pairs, and sometimes they offered him employment of an unspecified nature. Though they assured him that it would be "interesting and well paid," he was then earning very good money on North Sea oil rigs, and was not tempted. It was now more than a decade since the last visitation, but he did not doubt that the Company still had him carefully stockpiled in its vast data banks at Langley—or wherever they were these days.

He was in his office on the forty-sixth floor of the Teague Tower—now dwarfed by Houston's later skyscrapers—when he received the assignment that was to make him famous. The date happened to be April 2nd, and at first Bradley thought that his occasional client Jeff Rawlings had got it a day late. Despite his awesome responsibilities as operations manager on the Hibernia Platform, Jeff was noted for his sense of humor. This time, he wasn't joking; yet it was quite a while before Jason could take his problem seriously.

"Do you expect me to believe," he said, "that your million-ton rig has been shut down . . . by an *octopus*?"

"Not the whole operation, of course—but Manifold 1—our best producer. Forty thou barrels a day. Five flowlines running into it, all going full blast. Until yesterday."

The Hibernia project, it suddenly occurred to Jason, had the same general design as an octopus. Tentacles—or pipelines—ran out along the seabed from the central body to the dozen wells that had been drilled three thousand meters through the oil-rich sandstone. Before they reached the main platform, the flowlines from several individual wells were combined at a production manifold—also on the seabed, nearly a hundred meters down.

Each manifold was an automated industrial complex the size of a large apartment building, containing all the specialized equipment needed to handle the high-pressure mixture of gas, oil, and water erupting from the reservoirs far below. Tens of millions of years ago, nature had created and stored this hidden treasure; it was no simple matter to wrest it from her grasp.

"Tell me exactly what happened."

"This circuit secure?"

"Of course."

"Three days ago we started getting erratic instrument readings. The flow was perfectly normal, so we weren't too worried. But then there was a sudden data cutoff; we lost all monitoring facilities. It was obvious that the main fiber-optic trunk had been broken, and of course the automatics shut everything down."

"No surge problems?"

"No; slug-catcher worked perfectly—for once."

"And then?"

"S.O.P.—we sent down a camera—Eyeball Mark 5. Guess what?"

"The batteries died."

"Nope. The umbilical got snagged in the external scaffolding, before we could even go inside to look around."

"What happened to the driver?"

"Well, the kitchen isn't completely mechanized, and Chef Dubois can always use some unskilled labor."

"So you lost the camera. What happened next?"

"We haven't lost it—we know *exactly* where it is—but all it shows are lots of fish. So we sent down a diver to untangle things—and to see what he could find."

"Why not an ROV?"

There were always several underwater robots—Remotely Operated Vehicles—on any offshore oilfield. The old days when human divers did all the work were long since past.

There was an embarrassed silence at the other end of the line.

"Afraid you'd ask me that. We've had a couple of accidents—two ROVs are being rebuilt—and the rest can't be spared from an emergency job on the Avalon platform."

"Not your lucky day, is it? So that's why you've called the Bradley Corporation—'No job too deep.' Tell me more."

"Spare me that beat-up slogan. Since the depth's only ninety meters, we sent down a diver, in standard heliox gear. Well—ever heard a man screaming in helium? Not a very nice noise . . .

"When we got him up and he was able to talk again, he said the entire rig was covered by an octopus. He swore it was a hundred meters across. That's ridiculous, of course—but there's no doubt it's a monster."

"However big it is, a small charge of dynamite should encourage it to move."

"Much too risky. *You* know the layout down there—after all, you helped install it!"

"If the camera's still working, doesn't it show the beast?"

"We did get a glimpse of a tentacle—but no way of judging its size. We think it's gone back inside—we're worried that it might rip out more cables."

"You don't suppose it's fallen in love with the plumbing?"

"Very funny. My guess is that it's found a free lunch. You know—the bloody Oasis Effect that Publicity's always boasting about."

Bradley did indeed. Far from being damaging to the environment, virtually all underwater artifacts were irresistibly attractive to marine life, and often became a target for fishing boats and a paradise for anglers. He sometimes wondered how fish had managed to survive, before mankind generously provided them with condominiums by scattering wrecks across the seabeds of the world.

"Perhaps a cattle prod would do the trick—or a heavy dose of subsonics."

"We don't care *how* it's done—as long as there's no damage to the equipment. Anyway, it looked like a job for you—and Jim, of course. Is he ready?"

"He's *always* ready."

"How soon can you get to St. John's? There's a Chevron jet at Dallas—it can pick you up in an hour. What does Jim weigh?"

"One point five tons."

"No problem. When can you be at the airport?"

"Give me three hours. This isn't my normal line of business—I'll have to do some research."

"Usual terms?"

"Yes—hundred K plus expenses."

"And no cure, no pay?"

Bradley smiled. The centuries-old salvage formula had probably never been invoked in a case like this, but it seemed applicable. And it would be an easy job. A hundred meters, indeed! What nonsense . . .

"Of course. Call you back in one hour to confirm. Meanwhile please fax the manifold plans, so I can refresh my memory."

"Right—and I'll see what else I can find out, while I'm waiting for your call."

There was no need to waste time packing; Bradley always had two bags ready—one for the tropics, one for the Arctic. The first was very little used; most of his jobs, it seemed, were in unpleasant parts of the world, and this one would be no exception. The North Atlantic at this time of year would be cold, and probably rough; not that it would matter much, a hundred meters down.

Those who thought of Jason Bradley as a tough, no-nonsense roughneck would have been surprised at his next action. He pressed a button on his desk console, lay back in his partially reclining chair, and closed his eyes. To all outward appearances, he was asleep.

It had been years before he discovered the identity of the haunting music that had ebbed and flowed across *Glomar Explorer*'s deck, almost half a lifetime ago. Even then, he had known it must have been inspired by the sea; the slow rhythm of the waves was unmistakable. And how appropriate that the composer was Russian—the most underrated of his country's three titans, seldom mentioned in the same breath as Tchaikovsky and Stravinsky . . .

As Sergey Rachmaninoff himself had done long ago, Jason Bradley had stood transfixed before Arnold Boecklin's "Isle of the Dead," and now he was seeing it again in his mind's eye. Sometimes he identified himself with the mysterious, shrouded figure standing in the boat; sometimes he was the oarsman (Charon?); and sometimes he was the sinister cargo, being carried to its last resting place beneath the cypresses.

It was a secret ritual that had somehow evolved over the years, and which he believed had saved his life more than once. For while he was engrossed in the music, his subconscious mind—which apparently had no interest in such trivialities—was very busy indeed, analyzing the job that lay ahead, and foreseeing problems that might arise. At least that was Bradley's more-than-half-seriously-held theory, which he never intended to disprove by too close an examination.

Presently he sat up, switched off the music module, and swung his seat around to one of his half-dozen keyboards. The NeXT Mark 4 which stored most of his files and information was hardly the last word in computers, but Bradley's business had grown up with it and he had resisted all updates, on the sound principle "If it works, don't fix it."

"I thought so," he muttered, as he scanned the encyclopedia entry "Octopus." "Maximum size when fully extended may be as much as ten meters. Weight fifty to one hundred kilograms."

Bradley had never seen an octopus even approaching this size, and like most divers he knew considered them charming and inoffensive creatures. That they could be aggressive, much less dangerous, was an idea he had never taken seriously.

"See also entry on 'Sports, Underwater.'"

He blinked twice at this last reference, instantly accessed it, and read it with a mixture of amusement and surprise. Although he had often tried his hand at sports diving, he had the typical professional's disdain for amateur scubanauts. Too many of them had approached him looking for jobs, blissfully unaware of the fact that most of his work was in water too deep for unprotected humans, often with zero light and even zero visibility.

But he had to admire the intrepid divers of Puget Sound, who wrestled with opponents heavier than themselves and with four times as many arms—and brought them back to the surface without injuring them. (That, it seemed, was one of the rules of the game; if you hurt your octopus before you put it back in the sea, you were disqualified.)

The encyclopedia's brief video sequence was the stuff of nightmares: Bradley wondered how well the Puget Sounders slept. But it gave him one vital piece of information.

How *did* these crazy sportsmen—and sportswomen, there

were plenty of them as well—persuade a peaceable mollusc to emerge from its lair and indulge in hand-to-tentacle combat? He could hardly believe that the answer was so simple.

Pausing only to place a couple of unusual orders with his regular supplier, he grabbed his travel kit and headed for the airport.

"Easiest hundred K I ever earned," Jason Bradley told himself.

11.
ADA

A CHILD WITH two brilliant parents has a double handicap, and the Craigs had made life even more difficult for their daughter by naming her Ada. This well-advertised tribute to the world's first computer theorist perfectly summed up their ambitions for the child's future; it would, they devoutly hoped, be happier than that of Lord Byron's tragic daughter: Ada, Lady Lovelace.

It was a great disappointment, therefore, when Ada showed no particular talent for mathematics. By the age of six, the Craigs' friends had joked, "She should at least have discovered the binomial theorem." As it was, she used her computer without showing any real interest in its operation; it was just another of the household gadgets, like vidphones, remote controllers, voice-operated systems, wall TV, colorfax . . .

Ada even seemed to have difficulty with simple logic, finding AND, NOR, and NAND gates quite baffling. She took an instant dislike to Boolean operators, and had been known to burst into tears at the sight of an IF/THEN statement.

"Give her time," Donald pleaded to the often impatient Edith. "There's nothing wrong with her intelligence. I was at least ten before I understood recursive loops. Maybe she's going to be an artist. Her last report gave her straight A's in painting, clay modeling—"

"And a D in arithmetic. What's worse, she doesn't seem to *care*! That's what I find so disturbing."

Donald did not agree, but he knew that it would only start another fight if he said so. He loved Ada too much to see any faults in her; as long as she was happy, and did reasonably well at school, that was all that mattered to him now. Sometimes he wished that they had not saddled her with that evocative name, but Edith still seemed determined to have a genius-type daughter. That was now the least of their disagreements. Indeed, if it had not been for Ada, they would have separated long ago.

"What are we going to do about the puppy?" he asked, eager to change the subject. "It's only three weeks to her birthday—and we promised."

"Well," said Edith, softening for a moment, "she still hasn't made up her mind. I only hope she doesn't choose something enormous—like a Great Dane. Anyway, it wasn't a promise. We told her it would depend on her next school test."

You told her, Donald thought. Whatever the result, Ada's going to get that puppy. Even if she wants an Irish wolfhound—which, after all, would be the appropriate dog for this huge estate.

Donald was still not sure if it was a good idea, but they could easily afford it, and he had long since given up arguing with Edith once she had made up her mind. She had been born and reared in Ireland, and she was determined that Ada should have the same advantage.

Conroy Castle had been neglected for over half a century, and some portions were now almost in ruins. But what was left was more than ample for a modern family, and the stables were in particularly good shape, having been maintained by a local riding school. After vigorous scrubbing and extensive chemical warfare, they provided excellent accommodation for computers and communications equipment. The local residents thought it was a very poor exchange.

On the whole, however, the locals were friendly enough. After all, Edith was an Irish girl who had made good, even if she had married an Englishman. And they heartily approved of the Craigs' efforts to restore the famous gardens to at least some vestige of their Nineteenth-Century glory.

One of Donald's first moves, after they had made the west-wing ground floor livable, was to repair the camera obscura whose dome was a late-Victorian afterthought (some said excrescence) on the castle battlements. It had been installed by Lord Francis Conroy, a keen amateur astronomer and telescope maker, during the last decade of his life; when he was paralyzed but too proud to be pushed around the estate in a wheelchair, he had spent hours surveying his empire from this vantage point—and issuing instructions to his army of gardeners by semaphore.

The century-old optics were still in surprisingly good condition, and threw a brilliant image of the outside world on to the horizontal viewing table. Ada was fascinated by the instrument and the sense of power it gave her as she scanned the castle grounds. It was, she declared, much better than TV—or the boring old movies her parents were always screening.

And up here on the battlements, she could not hear the sound of their angry voices.

12.
A
MOLLUSC
OF
UNUSUAL
SIZE

THE FIRST BAD NEWS came soon after Bradley had settled down to his belated lunch. Chevron Canada fed its VIPs well, and Jason knew that as soon as he hit St. John's he'd have little time for leisurely, regular meals.

"Sorry to bother you, Mr. Bradley," said the steward, "but there's an urgent call from Head Office."

"Can't I take it from here?"

"I'm afraid not—there's video as well. You'll have to go back."

"Damn," said Bradley, taking one quick mouthful of a splendid piece of Texas steak. He reluctantly pushed his plate aside, and walked to the communications booth at the rear of the jet. The video was only one way, so he had no compunction about continuing to chew as Rawlings gave his report.

"We've been doing some research, Jason, about octopus sizes—the people out on the platform weren't very happy when you laughed at their estimate."

"Too bad. I've checked with my encyclopedia. The very *largest* octopus is under ten meters across."

"Then you'd better look at this."

Though the image that flashed on the screen was obviously a very old photograph, it was of excellent quality. It showed a group of men on a beach, surrounding a shapeless mass about the size of an elephant. Several other photos followed in quick succession; they were all equally clear, but of *what* it was impossible to say.

"If I had to put any money on it," said Bradley, "my guess would be a badly decomposed whale. I've seen—and smelled— several. They look just like that; unless you're a marine biologist, you could never identify it. That's how sea serpents get born."

"Nice try, Jason. That's exactly what most of the experts said at the time—which, by the way, was 1896. And the place was Florida—Saint Augustine Beach, to be precise."

"My steak is getting cold, and this isn't exactly helping my appetite."

"I won't take much longer. That little morsel weighed about five tons; luckily, a piece was preserved in the Smithsonian, so that fifty years later scientists were able to reexamine it. There's no doubt that it *was* an octopus; and it must have had a span of almost seventy meters. So our diver's guess of a hundred may not have been all that far out."

Bradley was silent for a few moments, processing this very unexpected—and unwelcome—piece of information.

"I'll believe it when I see it," he said, "though I'm not sure that I want to."

"By the way," said Rawlings, "you haven't mentioned this to anyone?"

"Of course not," snapped Jason, annoyed at the very suggestion.

"Well, the media have got hold of it somehow; the newsfax headlines are already calling it Oscar."

"Good publicity; what are you worried about?"

"We'd hoped you could get rid of the beast without everyone looking over your shoulder. Now we've got to be careful; mustn't hurt dear little Oscar. The World Wildlife people are watching. Not to mention Bluepeace."

"Those crazies!"

"Maybe. But WW has to be taken seriously; remember who they have as president. We don't want to upset the palace."

"I'll do my best to be gentle. Definitely no nukes—not even a small one."

The first bite of his now tepid steak triggered a wry memory. Several times, Bradley recalled, he had eaten octopus—and quite enjoyed it.

He hoped he could avoid the reverse scenario.

13.
PYRAMID
POWER

WHEN THE SOBBING ADA had been sent to her room, Edith and Donald Craig stared at each other in mutual disbelief.

"I don't understand it," said Edith at last. "She's never been disobedient before; in fact, she always got on very well with Miss Ives."

"And this is just the sort of test she's usually very good at—no equations, only multiple choices and pretty pictures. Let me read that note again. . . ."

Edith handed it over, while continuing to study the examination paper that had caused all the trouble.

Dear Mr. Craig,

I am very sorry to say that I have had to suspend Ada for insubordination.

This morning her class was given the attached Standard Visual Perception Test. She did extremely well (95%) with all the problems except Number 15. To my surprise, she was the *only* member of the class to give an incorrect answer to this very simple question.

When this was pointed out to her, she flatly denied that she was wrong. Even when I showed her the printed answer, she refused to admit her mistake and stubbornly maintained that everyone else was in error! At this point it became necessary, for the sake of class discipline, to send her home.

I am truly sorry, as she is usually such a good girl. Perhaps you will talk to her and make her see reason.

Sincerely,
Elizabeth Ives (Head Mistress)

"It almost looks," said Donald, "as if she was *deliberately* trying to fail."

Edith shook her head. "I don't think so. Even with this mistake, she'd have got a good pass."

Donald stared at the little set of brightly colored geometrical figures that had caused all the trouble.

"There's only one thing to do," he said. "You go and talk to her and calm her down. Give me ten minutes with a scissors and some stiff paper—then I'll settle it once and for all, so there can't be any further argument."

"I'm afraid that will only be tackling the symptoms, not the disease. We want to know *why* she kept insisting she was right. That's almost *pathological*. We may have to send her to a psychiatrist."

The thought had already occurred to Donald, but he had instantly rejected it. In later years, he would often remember the irony of this moment.

While Edith was consoling Ada, he quickly measured out the necessary triangles with pencil and ruler, cut them from the paper, and joined up the edges until he had made three examples of the two simplest possible solid figures—two tetrahedrons, one pyramid, all with equal sides. It seemed a childish exercise, but it was the least he could do for his beloved and troubled daughter.

15 (a) [he read]. Here are two identical tetrahedrons. Each has 4 equilateral triangles for sides, making a total of 8.

If any of the two faces are placed together, how many sides does the new solid have?

It was such a simple thought experiment that any child should be able to do it. Since two of the eight sides were swallowed up in the resulting diamond-shaped solid, the answer was obviously six. At least Ada had got *that* right. . . .

Holding it between thumb and first finger, Donald spun the little cardboard diamond a few times, then dropped it on his desk with a sigh. It split apart at once into the two components.

15 (b). Here are a tetrahedron and a pyramid, each with edges of the same length. The pyramid, however, has a *square* base as well as 4 triangular sides. Altogether, therefore, the two figures have 9 sides.

If any two of the triangular faces are placed in contact, how many sides does the resulting figure have?

"Seven, of course," Donald muttered, since two of the original nine will be lost inside the new solid. . . .

Idly, he tilted the little cardboard shapes until a pair of triangles merged.

Then he blinked.

Then his jaw dropped.

He sat in silence for a moment, checking the evidence of his own eyes. A slow smile spread across his face, and he said quietly into the housecom: "Edith—Ada—I've got something to show you."

The moment Ada entered, red-eyed and still sniffling, he reached out and took her in his arms.

"Ada," he whispered, stroking her hair gently, "I'm very proud of you." The astonishment on Edith's face delighted him more than it should have.

"I wouldn't have believed it," he said. "The answer was so obvious that the people who set the paper never bothered to check it. Look . . ."

He took the five-sided pyramid and stuck the four-sided tetrahedron on one face.

The new shape had only five sides—not the "obvious" seven. . . .

"Even though I've found the answer," Donald continued— and there was something like awe in his voice as he looked at his now smiling daughter—"I can't *visualize* it mentally. How did you *know* that the other sides lined up like this?"

Ada looked puzzled.

"What else could they do?" she answered.

There was a long silence while Donald and Edith absorbed this reply, and almost simultaneously came to the same conclusion.

Ada might have little comprehension of logic or analysis— but her feeling for space—her geometrical intuition—was altogether extraordinary. At the age of nine, it was certainly far superior to that of her parents. Not to mention those who had set the examination paper. . . .

The tension in the room slowly drained away. Edith began

to laugh, and presently all three of them embraced with almost childlike joy.

"Poor Miss Ives!" chortled Donald. "Wait until we tell her that she's got the Ramanujan of geometry in her class!"

It was one of the last happy moments of their married life; they would often cling to its memory in the bitter years to come.

14.
CALLING
ON OSCAR

"WHY ARE THESE THINGS always called Jim?" said the reporter who had intercepted Bradley at St. John's Airport. He was surprised there was only one, considering the excitement his mission seemed to be generating. One, of course, was often more than enough; but at least there was no Bluepeace demonstration to contend with.

"After the first diver who wore an armored suit, when they salvaged the *Lusitania*'s gold back in the thirties. Of course, they've been enormously improved since then. . . ."

"How?"

"Well, they're self-propelled, and I could live in Jim for fifty hours, two kilometers down—though it wouldn't be much fun. Even with servo-assisted limbs, four hours is maximum efficient working time."

"You wouldn't get *me* into one of those things," said the reporter, as the fifteen hundred kilos of titanium and plastic that had accompanied Bradley from Houston was being carefully hoisted into a Chevron helicopter. "Just *looking* at it gives me claustrophobia. Especially when you remember—"

Bradley knew what was coming, and escaped by waving goodbye and walking toward the chopper. The question had been put to him, in one form or another, by at least a dozen interviewers hoping to get some reaction. They had all been disappointed, and had been forced to concoct such imaginative headlines as THE IRON MAN IN THE TITANIUM SUIT.

"Aren't you afraid of ghosts?" he had been asked—even by other divers. They were the only people he had answered seriously.

"Why should I be?" he had always replied. "Ted Collier was my best friend; God alone knows how many drinks we shared." ("And girls," he might have added.) "Ted would have been delighted; no other way I could have afforded Jim back in those days—got him for a quarter of what he'd cost to build. State of the art, too—never had a mechanical failure. Sheer bad luck Ted was trapped before they could get him out from that collapsed rig. And you know . . . Jim kept him alive three hours longer than the guarantee. Someday I may need those three hours myself."

But not, he hoped, on this job—if his secret ingredient worked. It was much too late to pull out now; he could only trust that his encyclopedia, which seemed to have let him down badly in one important detail, had been accurate in other matters.

As always, Jason was impressed by the sheer size of the Hibernia platform, even though only a fraction of it was visible above sea level. The million-ton concrete island looked like a fortress, its jagged outline giving a field of fire in all directions. And indeed it was designed to ward off an implacable, though nonhuman, enemy—the great bergs that came drifting down from their Arctic nursery. The engineers claimed that the structure could withstand the maximum possible impact. Not everyone believed them.

There was a slight delay as the helicopter approached the landing platform on the roof of the multistoried topside building; it was already occupied by an RAF chopper, which had to be rolled aside before they could touch down. Bradley took one glance at its insignia, and groaned silently. How *did* they know so quickly? he wondered.

The president of World Wildlife was waiting for him as soon as he stepped out onto the windswept platform, and the big rotors came slowly to rest.

"Mr. Bradley? I know your reputation, of course—I'm delighted to meet you."

"Er—thank you, Your Highness."

"This octopus—is it *really* as big as they say?"

"That's what I intend to find out."

"Better you than me. And how do you propose to deal with it?"

"Ah—that's a trade secret."

"Nothing violent, I hope."

"I've already promised not to use nukes . . . sir."

The Prince gave a fleeting smile, then pointed to the somewhat battered fire extinguisher which Bradley was carefully nursing.

"You must be the first diver to carry one of *those* things underwater. Are you going to use it like a hypodermic syringe? Suppose the patient objects?"

Not a bad guess, thought Bradley; give him six out of ten. And I'm not a British citizen; he can't send me to the Tower for refusing to answer questions.

"Something like that, Your Highness. And it won't do any permanent harm."

I hope, he added silently. There were other possibilities;

Oscar might be completely indifferent—or he might get annoyed. Bradley was confident that he would be perfectly safe inside Jim's metal armor, but it would be uncomfortable to be rattled around like a pea in a pod.

The Prince still seemed worried, and Bradley felt quite certain that his concern was not for the human protagonist in the coming encounter. His Royal Highness's words quickly confirmed that suspicion.

"Please remember, Mr. Bradley, that this creature is unique—this is the first time anybody has ever seen one alive. And it's probably the largest animal in the world. *Perhaps the largest that's ever existed.* Oh, some dinosaurs certainly weighed more—but they didn't cover as much territory."

Bradley kept thinking of those words as he sank slowly toward the seabed, and the pale North Atlantic sunlight faded to complete blackness. They exhilarated rather than alarmed him; he would not have been in this business if he scared easily. And he felt that he was not alone; two benign ghosts were riding with him into the deep.

One was the first man ever to experience this world—his boyhood hero William Beebe, who had skirted the edge of the abyss in his primitive bathysphere, back in the 1930s. And the other was Ted Collier, who had died in the very space that Bradley was occupying now—quietly, and without fuss, because there was nothing else to do.

"Bottom coming up; visibility about twenty meters—can't see the installation yet."

Topside, everyone would be watching him on sonar and—as soon as he reached it—through the snagged camera.

"Target at thirty meters, bearing two two zero."

"I see it; current must have been stronger than I thought. Hitting the deck now."

For a few seconds everything was hidden in a cloud of silt,

and—as he always did at such moments—he recalled Apollo 11's
"Kicking up a little dust." The current swiftly cleared the
obscuring haze, and he was able to survey the massive engineering complex now looming up in the twin beams from Jim's
external lights.

It seemed that a fair-sized chemical factory had been
dumped on the seabed, to become a rendezvous for myriads of
fish. Bradley could see less than a quarter of the whole
installation, as most of it was hidden in distance and darkness.
But he knew the layout intimately, for he had spent a good deal
of expensive, frustrating, and occasionally dangerous time in
almost identical rigs.

A massive framework of steel tubes, thicker than a man,
formed an open cage around an assembly of valves, pipes, and
pressure vessels, threaded with cables and miscellaneous minor
plumbing. It looked as if it had been thrown together without
rhyme or reason, but Bradley knew that every item had been
carefully planned to deal with the immense forces slumbering far
below.

Jim had no legs—underwater, as in space, they were often
more of a nuisance than they were worth—and his movements
could be controlled with exquisite precision by low-powered
jets. It had been more than a year since Bradley had worn his
mobile armor, and at first he overcorrected, but old skills
quickly reasserted themselves.

He let himself drift gently toward his objective, hovering a
few centimeters above the seabed to avoid stirring up silt. This
was a situation where good visibility was important, and he was
glad that Jim's hemispheric dome gave him an all-around view.

Remembering the fate of the camera—it lay a few meters
away in a tangle of pencil-thin cabling—Bradley paused just
outside the framework of the manifold, considering the best
way of getting inside. His first objective was to find the break in

the fiber-optic monitor link; he knew its exact routing, so this should not present any problems.

His second was to evict Oscar; that might not be quite so easy.

"Here we go," he reported to topside. "Coming in through the tradesman's entrance—Access Tunnel B . . . not much room to maneuver, but no problem. . . ."

He scraped once, very gently, against the metal walls of the circular corridor, and as he did so became aware of a steady, low-frequency *thump, thump, thump* . . . coming from somewhere in the labyrinth of tanks and tubes around him. Presumably some piece of equipment was still functioning; it must have been very much noisier around here when everything was running full blast. . . .

The thought triggered a long-forgotten memory. He recalled how, as a small boy, he had silenced the speakers of a local fairground's PA system with well-aimed shots from his father's rifle—and had then lived for weeks in fear of being found out. Maybe Oscar had also been offended by this noisy intruder into his domain, and had taken similar direct action to restore peace and quiet.

But where *was* Oscar?

"I'm puzzled—I'm right inside now, and can see the whole layout. Plenty of hiding places—but none of them big enough to conceal anything larger than a man. Certainly nothing as big as an elephant! Ah—this is what you're looking for!"

"What have you found?"

"Main cable trunk—looks like a plate of spaghetti that's been dropped by a careless waiter. Must have taken some strength to rip it open; you'll have to replace the whole section."

"What could have done it? Hungry shark?"

"Or angry moray eel. But no teeth marks—I'd expect

some. And teeth, for that matter. An occi's still the best bet. But whoever did it isn't at home."

Taking his time, Bradley made a careful survey of the installation, and could find no other sign of damage. With any luck, the unit should be operational within a couple of days—unless the secret saboteur struck again. Meanwhile, there was nothing more that he could do; he began to jet his way delicately back the way he had come, steering Jim in and out of the maze of girders and pipes. Once he disturbed a small, pulpy mass that was indeed an octopus—perhaps as much as a meter across.

"Cross *you* off my list of suspects," he muttered to himself.

He was almost through the outer framework of massive tubes and girders when he realized that the scenery had changed.

Many years ago, he had been a reluctant small boy on a school tour of a famous botanical garden in southern Georgia. He remembered practically nothing of the visit, but there was one item that, for some reason, had impressed him greatly. He had never heard of the banyan, and was amazed to discover that there was a tree that could have not one trunk, but dozens—each a separate pillar serving to support its widespread canopy of branches.

In the present case, of course, there were exactly eight, though he did not bother to count them. He was staring into the huge, jet-black eyes, like fathomless pools of ink, that were regarding him dispassionately.

Bradley had often been asked "Have you ever been frightened?" and had always given the same answer: "God, yes—many times. But always when it was over—that's why I'm still around." Though no one would ever believe it, he was not in the least frightened now—only awed, as any man might be by some unexpected wonder. Indeed, his first reaction was: "I owe an apology to that diver." His second was: "Let's see if this works."

The cylinder of the fire extinguisher was already grasped by Jim's left external manipulator, and Bradley servoed it up toward the aiming position. Simultaneously, he moved the right limb so that its mechanical fingers could work the trigger. The whole operation took only seconds; but Oscar reacted first.

He seemed to be mimicking Bradley's actions, aiming a tube of flesh toward him—almost as if imitating his hastily modified fire extinguisher. Is he going to squirt something at *me*? Bradley wondered. . . .

He would never have believed that anything so big could move so quickly. Even inside his armor, Bradley felt the impact of the jet-stream, as Oscar switched to emergency drive; this was no time for walking along the seabed like an eight-legged table. Then everything disappeared in a cloud of ink so dense that Jim's high-intensity lights were completely useless.

On his leisurely way back to the surface, Bradley whispered softly to his dead friend: "Well, Ted, we did it again—but I don't think we can take much credit."

Judging by the manner of his going, he did not believe that Oscar would return. He could see the animal's point of view—even sympathize with it.

There the peaceable mollusc was, quietly going about his business of preventing the North Atlantic from becoming a solid mass of cod. Suddenly, out of nowhere, appeared a monstrous apparition blazing with lights and waving ominous appendages. Oscar had done what any intelligent octopus would do. He had recognized that there was a creature in the sea much more ferocious than himself.

"My congratulations, Mr. Bradley," said H.R.H. as Jason slowly emerged from his armor. This was always a difficult and undignified operation, but it kept him in good shape. If he put on another couple of centimeters, he would never be able to squeeze through the O-ring of the helmet seal.

"Thank you, sir," he replied. "All part of the day's work."
The Prince chuckled.

"I thought we British had a monopoly on understatement. And I don't suppose you're prepared to reveal your secret ingredient?"

Jason smiled and shook his head.

"One day I may need to use it again."

"Whatever it was," said Rawlings with a grin, "it cost us a pretty penny. When we tracked him on sonar—amazing what a feeble echo he gives—Oscar was certainly moving fast toward deep water. But suppose he comes back when he gets hungry again? There's nowhere else in the North Atlantic where the fishing's so good."

"I'll make a deal with you," Jason answered, pointing to his battered cylinder. "If he does, I'll rush you my magic bullet—and you can send down your own man to deal with him. It won't cost you a cent."

"There's a catch somewhere," said Rawlings. "It can't be that easy."

Jason smiled, but did not answer. Though he was playing strictly by the rules, he felt a slight—very slight—twinge of conscience. The "No cure, no pay" slogan also implied that you got paid when you effected a cure, no questions asked. He had earned his hundred K bucks, and if anyone ever asked him how it was done, he would answer: "Didn't you know? An octopus is easy to hypnotize."

There was only one mild cause for dissatisfaction. He wished he'd had a chance of checking the household hint in the old Jacques Cousteau book that his encyclopedia had providentially quoted. It would be interesting to know if *Octopus giganteus* had the same aversion to concentrated copper sulphate as his midget ten-meter cousin, *Octopus vulgaris*.

15.
CONROY
CASTLE

The Mandelbrot Set—hereinafter referred to as the M-Set—is one of the most extraordinary discoveries in the entire history of mathematics. That is a rash claim, but we hope to justify it.

The stunning beauty of the images it generates means that its appeal is both emotional and universal. Invariably these images bring gasps of astonishment from those who have never encountered them before; we have seen people almost hypnotized by the computer-produced films that explore its—quite literally—infinite ramifications.

Thus it is hardly surprising that within a decade of Benoit Mandelbrot's 1980 discovery it began to have an impact on the visual arts and crafts, such as the designs of fabrics, carpets, wallpaper, and even jewelry. And, of course, the Hollywood dream factories were soon using it (and its relatives) twenty-four hours a day. . . .

The psychological reasons for this appeal are still a mystery, and may always remain so; perhaps there is some structure, if one can use that term, in the human mind that resonates to the patterns in the M-Set. Carl Jung would have been surprised—and delighted—to know that thirty years after his death, the computer revolution whose beginnings he just lived to see would give new impetus to his theory of archetypes and his belief in the existence of a "collective unconscious." Many patterns in the M-Set are strongly reminiscent of Islamic art; perhaps the best example is the familiar comma-shaped "Paisley" design. But there are other shapes that remind one of organic structures—tentacles, compound insect eyes, armies of seahorses, elephant trunks . . . then, abruptly, they become transformed into the crystals and snowflakes of a world before any life began.

Yet perhaps the most astonishing feature of the M-Set is its basic simplicity. Unlike almost everything else in modern mathematics, any schoolchild can understand how it is produced. Its generation involves nothing more advanced than addition and multiplication; it does not even require subtraction or division, much less any higher functions. . . .

In principle—though not in practice!—it could have been discovered as soon as men learned to count. But even if they never grew tired, and never made a mistake, all the human beings who have ever existed would not have sufficed to do the elementary arithmetic required to produce an M-Set of quite modest magnification. . . .

(From "The Psychodynamics of the M-Set," by Edith and Donald Craig, in Essays Presented to

Professor Benoit Mandelbrot on his 80th Birthday:
MIT Press, 2004.)

"Are we paying for the dog, or the pedigree?" Donald
Craig had asked in mock indignation when the impressive sheet
of parchment had arrived. "She's even got a coat of arms, for
heaven's sake!"

It had been love at first sight between Lady Fiona McDon-
ald of Glen Abercrombie—a fluffy half-kilogram of Cairn
terrier—and the nine-year-old girl. To the surprise and disappointment of the neighbors, Ada had shown no interest in
ponies. "Nasty, smelly things," she told Patrick O'Brian, the
head gardener, "with a bite at one end and a kick at the other."
The old man had been shocked at so unnatural a reaction from
a young lady, especially one who was half Irish at that.

Nor was he altogether happy with some of the new owners'
projects for the estate on which his family had worked for five
generations. Of course, it was wonderful to have *real* money
flowing into Conroy Castle again, after decades of poverty—but
converting the stables into computer rooms! It was enough to
drive a man to drink, if he wasn't there already.

Patrick had managed to derail some of the Craigs' more
eccentric ideas by a policy of constructive sabotage, but they—
or rather Miz Edith—had been adamant about the remodeling of
the lake. After it had been dredged and some hundreds of tons
of water hyacinth removed, she had presented Patrick with an
extraordinary map.

"*This* is what I want the lake to look like," she said, in a
tone that Patrick had now come to recognize all too well.

"What's it supposed to be?" he asked, with obvious dis-
taste. "Some kind of bug?"

"You could call it that," Donald had answered, in his

don't-blame-me-it's-all-Edith's-idea voice. "The Mandelbug.
Get Ada to explain it to you someday."

A few months earlier, O'Brian would have resented that
remark as patronizing, but now he knew better. Ada was a
strange child, but she was some kind of genius. Patrick sensed
that both her brilliant parents regarded her as much with awe as
with admiration. And he liked Donald considerably more than
Edith; for an Englishman, he wasn't too bad.

"The lake's no problem. But moving all those grown
cypress trees—I was only a boy when they were planted! It may
kill them. I'll have to talk it over with the Forestry Department
in Dublin."

"How long will it take?" asked Edith, totally ignoring his
objections.

"Do you want it quick, cheap, or good? I can give you any
two."

This was now an old joke between Patrick and Donald, and
the answer was the one they both expected.

"Fairly quick—and *very* good. The mathematician who
discovered this is in his eighties, and we'd like him to see it as
soon as possible."

"Nothing *I'd* be proud of discovering."

Donald laughed. "This is only a crude first approximation.
Wait until Ada shows you the real thing on the computer; you'll
be surprised."

I very much doubt it, thought Patrick.

The shrewd old Irishman was not often wrong. This was
one of the rare occasions.

16.
THE
KIPLING
SUITE

JASON BRADLEY and Roy Emerson had a good deal in common, thought Rupert Parkinson. They were both members of an endangered, if not dying species—the self-made American entrepreneur who had created a new industry or become the leader of an old one. He admired, but did not envy them; he was quite content, as he often put it, to have been "born in the business."

His choice of the Kipling Suite at Brown's for this meeting had been quite deliberate, though he had no idea how much, or how little, his guests knew about the writer. In any event, both Emerson and Bradley seemed impressed by the *ambience* of the room, with the historic photographs around the wall, and the very desk on which the great man had once worked.

"I never cared much for T. S. Eliot," began Parkinson, "until I came across his *Choice of Kipling's Verse*. I remember telling my Eng. Lit. tutor that a poet who liked Kipling couldn't be all bad. He wasn't amused."

"I'm afraid," said Bradley, "I've never read much poetry. Only thing of Kipling's I know is 'If—'"

"Pity: he's just the man for you—the poet of the sea, *and* of engineering. You really *must* read 'McAndrew's Hymn'; even though its technology's a hundred years obsolete, no one's ever matched its tribute to machines. And he wrote a poem about the deep sea cables that you'll appreciate. It goes:

"The wrecks dissolve above us; their dust drops down from afar—
Down to the dark, to the utter dark, where the blind white sea-snakes are.
There is no sound, no echo of sound, in the deserts of the deep,
Or the great grey level plains of ooze where the shell-burred cables creep."

"I like it," said Bradley. "But he was wrong about 'no echo of sound.' The sea's a very noisy place—if you have the right listening gear."

"Well, he could hardly have known *that*, back in the Nineteenth Century. He'd have been absolutely fascinated by our project—especially as he wrote a novel about the Grand Banks."

"He did?" both Emerson and Bradley exclaimed simultaneously.

"Not a very good one—nowhere near *Kim*—but what is? *Captains Courageous* is about the Newfoundland fishermen and their hard lives; Hemingway did a much better job, half a century later and twenty degrees further south. . . ."

"I've read *that*," said Emerson proudly. "*The Old Man and the Sea*."

"Top of the class, Roy. I've always thought it a tragedy that Kipling never wrote an epic poem about *Titanic*. Maybe he intended to, but Hardy beat him to it."

"Hardy?"

"Never mind. Please excuse us, Rudyard, while we get down to business. . . ."

Three flat display panels (and how *they* would have fascinated Kipling!) flipped up simultaneously. Glancing at his, Rupert Parkinson began: "We have your report dated thirtieth April. I assume that you've had no further inputs since then?"

"Nothing important. My staff has rechecked all the figures. We think we could improve on them—but we prefer to be conservative. I've never known a major underwater operation that didn't have some surprises."

"Even your famous encounter with Oscar?"

"Biggest surprise of all. Went even better than I'd expected."

"What about the status of *Explorer*?"

"No change, Rupe. She's still mothballed in Suisun Bay."

Parkinson flinched slightly at the "Rupe." At least it was better than "Parky"—permitted only to intimate friends.

"It's hard to believe," said Emerson, "that such a valuable—such a *unique*—ship has only been used once."

"She's too big to run economically, for any normal commercial project. Only the CIA could afford her—and it got its wrist slapped by Congress."

"I believe they once tried to hire her to the Russians."

Bradley looked at Parkinson, and grinned. "So you know about that?"

"Of course. We did a lot of research before we came to you."

"I'm lost," said Emerson. "Fill me in, please."

"Well, back in 1989 one of their newest Russian submarines—"

"Only Mike class they ever built."

"—sank in the North Sea, and some bright chappie in the

Pentagon said: 'Hey—perhaps we can get some of our money back!' But nothing ever came of it. Or *did* it, Jason?"

"Well, it wasn't the Pentagon's idea; no one there with that much imagination. But I can tell you that I spent a pleasant week in Geneva with the deputy director of the CIA and three admirals—one of ours, two of theirs. That was . . . ah, in the spring of 1990. Just when the Reformation was starting, so everyone lost interest. Igor and Alexei resigned to go into the export-import business; I still get Xmas cards every year from their office in Lenin—I mean Saint Pete. As you said, nothing ever came of the idea; but we all put on about ten kilos and took weeks to get back into shape."

"I know those Geneva restaurants. If you had to get *Explorer* shipshape, how long would it take?"

"If I can pick the men, three to four months. That's the only time estimate I can be sure of. Getting down to the wreck, checking its integrity, building any additional structural supports, getting your billions of glass balloons down to it—frankly, even those *maximum* figures I've put in brackets are only guesstimates. But I'll be able to refine them after the initial survey."

"That seems very reasonable: I appreciate your frankness. At this stage, all we really want to know is whether the project is even *feasible*—in the time frame."

"Timewise—yes. Costwise—who knows? What's your ceiling, anyway?"

Rupert Parkinson pretended to wince at the bluntness of the question.

"We're still doing our sums—aren't we, Roy?"

Some signal passed between them that Bradley could not interpret, but Emerson gave a clue with his reply.

"I'm still prepared to match anything the board puts up, Rupert. If the operation succeeds, I'll get it all back on Plan B."

"And what, may I ask, is Plan B?" said Bradley. "For that matter, what's Plan A? You still haven't told me what you intend to do with the hull, when you've towed it to New York. Do a *Vasa?*"

Parkinson threw up his hands in mock dismay. "He's guessed Plan C," he said with a groan. "Yes, we had thought of putting her on display, after we'd brought her into Manhattan— a hundred years behind schedule. But you know what happens to an iron ship when it's brought to the surface after a few decades underwater—preserving a *wooden* one is bad enough. Pickling *Titanic* in the right chemicals would take decades—and probably cost more than raising her."

"So you'll leave her in shallow water. Which means you'll be taking her to Florida, just as that TV show suggested."

"Look, Jason—we're still exploring *all* options: Disney World is only one of them. We won't even be disappointed if we have to leave her on the bottom—as long as we can salvage what's in Great-Grandfather's suite. It's lucky he refused to let all those chests be carried as cargo; his very last marconigram complained that he had no space for entertaining."

"And you're confident that all that fragile glass will still be intact?"

"Ninety percent of it. The Chinese discovered centuries ago that their wares could travel safely the length of the Silk Road—if they were packed in tea leaves. No one found anything better until polystyrene foam came along; and of course you can sell the tea, and make a nice profit on that as well."

"I doubt it, for this particular consignment."

"Afraid you're right. Pity—it was a personal gift from Sir Thomas Lipton—the very best from his Ceylon estates."

"You're quite sure it would have absorbed the impact?"

"Easily. The ship plowed into soft mud at an angle, doing

about thirty knots. Average deceleration two gee—maximum five."

Rupert Parkinson folded down the display panel and clicked shut the miracle of electronic intelligence which was now as casually accepted as the telephone had been a lifetime earlier.

"We'll call you again before the end of the week, Jason," continued Parkinson. "There's a board meeting tomorrow, and I hope it will settle matters. Again, many thanks for your report; *if* we decide to go ahead, can we count on you?"

"In what way?"

"As O.i.C. operations, of course."

There was a long pause; a little too long, Parkinson thought.

"I'm flattered, Rupe. I'd have to think it over—see how I could fit it into my schedule."

"Really, Jason—you wouldn't have any 'schedule' if this goes ahead. It's the biggest job you'll ever be offered." He almost added "Perhaps it's too big," but then thought better of it. Jason Bradley was not the sort of man one cared to annoy, especially if one hoped to do business with him.

"I quite agree," Bradley said, "and I'd like to take it on. Not just for the cash—which I'm sure will be okay—but the challenge. Win or lose. Very nice meeting you both—gotta run."

"Aren't you seeing *anything* of London? I can get you tickets to the new Andrew Lloyd Webber–Stephen King show. There aren't many people who can make that claim."

Bradley laughed. "Love to go—but they've managed to total a slugcatcher in the Orkneys field, and I've promised to be in Aberdeen by this afternoon."

"Very well. We'll keep in touch. . . ."

"What do you think, Roy?" Parkinson asked, when the room was quiet again.

"Tough little guy, isn't he? Do you suppose he's holding out for the highest bidder?"

"That's just what I was wondering. If he is, he'll be out of luck."

"Oh—our legal eagles have done their thing?"

"Almost; there are still some loose ends. Remember when I took you to Lloyd's?"

"I certainly do."

It had indeed been a memorable occasion for an out-of-town visitor; even in this twenty-first century, the "new" Lloyd's building still looked positively futuristic. But what had most impressed Emerson had been the Casualty Book—the register of wrecks. That series of massive volumes recorded all the most dramatic moments in maritime history. Their guide had shown them the page for 15 April 1912, and the copperplate handwriting encapsulating the news that had just stunned the world.

Heart-stopping though it was to read those words, they had less impact on Roy Emerson than an awesome triviality he noticed when skimming through the earlier volumes.

All the entries, spanning a period of more than two hundred years, seemed to be in the same handwriting. It was an example of tradition and continuity that would be very hard to beat.

"Well, Dad's been a member of Lloyd's for ages, so we have—ah—a certain influence there."

"*That* I can well believe."

"Thank you. Anyway, the board's had some discussions with the International Seabed Authority. There are dozens of conflicting claims, and the lawyers are doing rather well. They're the only ones who can't lose—whatever happens."

Roy Emerson sometimes found Rupert's discursiveness exasperating; he never seemed in a hurry to get to the point. It was hard to believe that he could act quickly in an emergency—yet he was one of the best yachtsmen in the world.

"It would be nice if we could claim exclusive ownership—after all, she was a British ship—"

"—built with American money—"

"A detail we'll overlook. At the moment, she doesn't belong to anyone, and it will have to be settled in the World Court. That could take years."

"We don't have years."

"Precisely. But we think we can get an injunction to stop anyone else trying to raise her—while we go ahead quietly with our own plans."

"Quietly! You must be joking. Know how many interviews I've turned down lately?"

"Probably about as many as I have." Rupert glanced at his watch. "Just in time. Like to see something interesting?"

"Of course." Emerson knew that whatever Parkinson called "interesting" was likely to be something he would never have another chance of seeing in his life. The *real* crown jewels, perhaps; or 21b Baker Street; or those books in the British Museum Library that were curiously named curious, and weren't listed in the main catalogue. . . .

"It's just across the road—we can walk there in two minutes. The Royal Institution. Faraday's lab—where most of our civilization was born. They were rearranging the exhibit when some clod managed to drop the retort he used when he discovered benzene. The director wants to know if we can match the glass, and repair it so that no one will ever notice."

It was not every day, Emerson told himself, that you had a chance of visiting Michael Faraday's laboratory. They crossed the narrow width of Albemarle Street, easily dodging the slow-moving traffic, and walked a few meters to the classical facade of the Royal Institution.

"Good afternoon, Mr. Parkinson. Sir Ambrose is expecting you."

17.
DEEP
FREEZE

"I HOPE YOU don't mind meeting us at the airport, Mrs. Craig . . . Donald . . . but the traffic into Tokyo is getting worse every day. Also, the fewer people who see us, the better. I'm sure you'll understand."

Dr. Kato Mitsumasa, the young president of Nippon-Turner, was, as usual, immaculately dressed in a Savile Row suit that would remain in style for the next twenty years. Also as usual, he was accompanied by two samurai clones who remained in the background and would not say a word during the entire proceedings. Donald had sometimes wondered if Japanese robotics had made even more advances than was generally realized.

"We have a few minutes before our other guest arrives, so I'd like to go over some details that only concern us. . . .

"First of all, we've secured the world cable and satellite rights for your smokeless version of *A Night to Remember,* for the first six months of '12, with an option of another six months' extension."

"Splendid," said Donald. "I didn't believe even you could manage it, Kato—but I should have known better."

"Thank you; it wasn't easy, as the porcupine said to his girlfriend."

During the years of his Western education—London School of Economics, then Harvard and Annenberg—Kato had developed a sense of humor that often seemed quite out of keeping with his present position. If Donald closed his eyes, he could hardly believe that he was listening to a native-born Japanese, so perfect was Kato's mid-Atlantic accent. But every so often he would produce some outrageous wisecrack that was uniquely his own, owing nothing to either East or West. Even when his jokes appeared to be in bad taste—which was not infrequent—Donald suspected that Kato knew exactly what he was doing. It encouraged people to underestimate him; and that could cause them to make very expensive mistakes.

"Now," said Kato briskly, "I'm happy to say that all our computer runs and tank tests are satisfactory. If I may say so, what we're going to do is unique, and will seize the imagination of the whole world. No one, but *no one* else, can even attempt to raise *Titanic* the way we're going to do!"

"Well, part of her. Why just the stern?"

"Several reasons—some practical, some psychological. It's much the smaller of the two portions—less than fifteen thousand tons. And it was the last to go under, with all the remaining people on deck still clinging to it. We'll intercut with the scenes from *A Night to Remember*. Thought of reshooting them—or colorizing the original—"

"No!" said both Craigs simultaneously.

Kato seemed taken aback. "After what *you've* already done to it? Ah, the inscrutable Occident! Anyway, since it's a night scene it's just as effective in b/w."

"There's another editing problem we've not resolved," said Edith abruptly. "*Titanic*'s dance band."

"What about it?"

"Well, in the movie it plays 'Nearer My God to Thee.'"

"So?"

"That's the myth—and it's utter nonsense. The band's job was to keep up the passengers' spirits, and prevent panic. The very *last* thing they'd play would be a doleful hymn. One of the ship's officers would have shot them if they'd tried."

Kato laughed. "I've often felt that way about dance bands. But what did they play?"

"A medley of popular tunes, probably ending with a waltz called 'Song of Autumn.'"

"I see. That's true to life—but we can't have *Titanic* sinking to a waltz tune, for heaven's sake. *Ars longa, vita brevis,* as MGM almost used to say. In this case, art wins, and life takes second place."

Kato glanced at his watch, then at one of the clones, who walked to the door and disappeared down the corridor. In less than a minute, he returned accompanied by a short, powerfully built man with the universal insignia of the global executive—a carryall bag in one hand, an electronic briefcase in the other.

Kato greeted him warmly.

"Very pleased to meet you, Mr. Bradley. Someone once said that punctuality is the thief of time. I've never believed it, and I'm glad you agree. Jason Bradley, meet Edith and Donald Craig."

As Bradley and the Craigs shook hands with the slightly distracted air of people who thought they should know each other, but weren't quite certain, Kato hastened to put the record straight.

"Jason is the world's number one ocean engineer—"

"Of course! That giant octopus—"

"Tame as a kitten, Mrs. Craig. Nothing to it."

"—while Edith and Donald make old movies as good as new—or better. Let me explain why I've brought you together, at such rather short notice."

Bradley smiled. "Not very hard to guess, Mr. Mitsumasa. But I'll be interested in the details."

"Of that I'm sure. All this, of course, is highly confidential."

"Of course."

"First we plan to raise the stern, and shoot a really spectacular TV special as it comes to the surface. Then we'll tow it to Japan, and make it part of a permanent exhibit at Tokyo-on-Sea. There'll be a three-hundred-sixty-degree theater, the audience sitting in lifeboats rocking on water—beautiful starry night—almost freezing—we'll give them topcoats, of course—and they'll see and *hear* the last minutes as the ship goes underwater. Then they can go down into the big tank and view the stern through observation windows at various levels. Though it's only about a third of the whole ship, it's so big that you can't see it all at one time; even with the distilled water we'll use, visibility will be less than a hundred meters. The wreck will just fade away into the distance—so why bring up any more? The viewers will have a perfect illusion of being on the bottom of the Atlantic."

"Well, that seems logical," said Bradley. "And, of course, the stern is the easiest part to raise. It's already badly smashed up—you could lift it in sections weighing only a few hundred tons, and assemble them later."

There was an awkward silence. Then Kato said: "That won't look very glamorous on TV, will it? No. We have more ambitious plans. This is the bit that's top secret. Even though the stern portion is smashed to pieces, we're going to bring it up in a single operation. *Inside an iceberg*. Don't you think that's poetic justice? One iceberg sank her—another will bring her back to the light of day."

If Kato expected his visitor to be surprised, he was disappointed. By this time, Bradley had heard just about every scheme for raising the *Titanic* that the ingenious mind of man and woman could conceive.

"Go on," he said. "You'll need quite a refrigeration plant, won't you?"

Kato gave a triumphant smile. "No—thanks to the latest breakthrough in solid-state physics. You've heard of the Peltier Effect?"

"Of course. The cooling you get when an electric current is passed through certain materials—I don't know exactly which. But every domestic icebox has depended on it since 2001, when the environmental treaties banned fluorocarbons."

"Exactly. Now, the common or kitchen Peltier system isn't very efficient, but it doesn't have to be as long as it quietly manufactures ice cubes without blasting holes in the poor old ozone layer. However, our physicists have discovered a new class of semiconductors—a spinoff from the *super*conductor revolution—that ups efficiency several times. Which means that every icebox in the world is obsolete, as of last week."

"I'm sure"—Bradley smiled—"that all the Japanese manufacturers are heartbroken."

"The scramble for the patent licenses is on right now. And we haven't overlooked the advertising tie-in—when the biggest ice cube in the world surfaces—carrying the *Titanic* inside it."

"I'm impressed. But what about the power supply?"

"That's another angle we hope to exploit—swords into plowshares, though the metaphor is a little farfetched in this case. We're planning to use a couple of decommissioned nuclear subs—one Russian, one U.S. They can generate all the megawatts we need—and from several hundred meters down, so they can operate through the worst Atlantic storms."

"And your time scale?"

"Six months to install the hardware on the seabed. Then two years of Peltier cooling. Remember—it's almost freezing down there. We only have to drop the temperature a couple of degrees, and our iceberg will start to form."

"And how will you stop it from floating up before you're ready?"

Kato smiled.

"Let's not go into details at this stage—but I can assure you our engineers have thought of that small item. Anyway, this is where you come in—if you want to."

Does he know about the Parkinsons? Bradley wondered. Very probably; and even if he's not certain, he'll have guessed that they've made an offer.

"Excuse me a moment," said Kato apologetically, turning away and opening his briefcase. When he faced his visitors again, barely five seconds later, he had been transformed into a pirate chief. Only the barely visible thread leading to the keyboard in his hand revealed that the eye patch he was wearing was very hi-tech indeed.

"I'm afraid this proves I'm not a genuine Japanese—bad manners, you know . . . my father still uses a laptop, late Ming Dynasty. But monocs are so much more convenient, and give such superb definition."

Bradley and the Craigs could not help smiling at each other. What Kato said was perfectly true; many portable video devices now used compact microscreens that weighed little more than a pair of spectacles and indeed were often incorporated in them. Although the monoc was only a centimeter in front of the eye, a clever system of lenses made the postage-stamp-sized image appear as large as desired.

This was splendid for entertainment purposes—but it was even more useful for businessmen, lawyers, politicians, and anyone who wanted to access confidential information in total privacy. There was no way of spying on another person's electronic monocle—short of tapping the same data stream. Its chief disadvantage was that excessive use led to new types of schizophrenia, quite fascinating to investigators of the "split-brain" phenomenon.

When Kato had finished his litany of megawatt-hours, calorie-tons, and degrees-per-month coefficients, Bradley sat for a moment silently processing the information that had been dumped into his brain. Many of the details were too technical to be absorbed at first contact, but that was unimportant; he could study them later. He did not doubt that the calculations would be accurate—but there might still be essential points that had been overlooked. He had seen that happen so many times. . . .

His instincts told him, however, that the plan was sound. He had learned to take first impressions seriously—*especially* when they were negative, even if he could not pinpoint the exact cause of his premonition. This time, there were no bad vibes. The project was fantastic—but it could work.

Kato was watching him covertly, obviously trying to gauge his reactions. I can be pretty inscrutable when I want to, thought Bradley. . . . Besides, I have my reputation to consider.

Then Kato, with the ghost of a smile, handed him a small slip of paper, folded in two. Bradley took his time opening it. When he saw the figures, he realized that even if the project was a total disaster, he need give no further thought to his professional career. In the natural course of events, it could not last many more years—and he had not saved this much in his entire lifetime.

"I'm flattered," he said quietly. "You're more than generous. But I still have some other business to settle, before I can give you a definite answer."

Kato looked surprised. "How long?" he asked, rather brusquely.

He thinks I'm still negotiating with someone else, thought Bradley. Which is perfectly true—

"Give me a week. But I can tell you right away—I'm quite sure no one will match your offer."

"I know," said Kato, closing his briefcase. "Any points you want to make—Edith, Donald?"

"No," said Edith, "you seem to have covered everything." Donald said nothing, but merely nodded in agreement. This is a strange partnership, Bradley told himself, and not a very happy one. He had taken an immediate liking to Donald, who seemed a warm, gentle sort of person. But Edith was tough and domineering—almost aggressive; she was obviously the boss.

"And how is that delightful child prodigy who happens to be your daughter?" Kato asked the Craigs as they were about to leave. "Please give her my love."

"We will," Donald replied. "Ada's fine, and enjoyed her trip to Kyoto. It made a change from exploring the Mandelbrot Set."

"And just what," asked Bradley, "is the Mandelbrot Set?"

"Much easier shown than described," answered Donald. "Why don't you visit us? We'd like to take you around our studio—wouldn't we, Edith? Especially if we'll be working together—as I hope we will."

Only Kato noticed Bradley's momentary hesitation. Then Bradley smiled and answered: "I'd enjoy that—I'm going to Scotland next week, and think I could fit it in. How old is your girl?"

"Ada's almost nine. But if you asked her age, she'd probably tell you 8.876545 years."

Bradley laughed. "She *does* sound a prodigy. I'm not sure I could face her."

"And this," said Kato, "is the man who scared away a fifty-ton octopus. I'll *never* understand these Americans."

18.
IN AN
IRISH
GARDEN

"WHEN I WAS a small boy," said Patrick O'Brian wistfully, "I used to love coming up here to watch the magic pictures. They seemed so much brighter—and more interesting—than the *real* world outside. No telly in those days, of course—and the traveling tent cinema only came to the village about once a month."

"Don't you believe a word, Jason," said Donald Craig. "Pat isn't really a hundred years old."

Though Bradley would have guessed seventy-five, O'Brian might well be in his eighties. So he must have been born in the 1930s—perhaps even the '20s. The world of his youth already seemed unimaginably remote; reality outdid storytelling exaggeration, even by Irish standards.

Pat shook his head sadly, as he continued pulling on the cord that rotated the big lens five meters above their heads. On the matte-white table around which they were standing, the lawns and flowerbeds and gravel paths of Conroy Castle performed a stately pirouette. Everything was unnaturally bright and clear, and Bradley could well imagine that to a boy this beautiful old machine must have transformed the familiar outside world into an enchanted fairyland.

"'Tis a shame, Mr. Bradley, that Master Donald doesn't know the truth when he hears it. I could tell him stories of the old lord—but what's the use?"

"You tell them to Ada, anyway."

"Sure—and *she* believes me, sensible girl."

"So do I—sometimes. Like those about Lord Dunsany."

"Only after you'd checked up on me with Father Mc-Mullen."

"Dunsany? The author?" asked Bradley.

"Yes. You've read him?"

"Er—no. But he was a great friend of Dr. Beebe—the first man to go down half a mile. That's how I know the name."

"Well, you should read his stories—especially the ones about the sea. Pat says he often came here, to play chess with Lord Conroy."

"Dunsany was grand master of Ireland," Patrick added. "But he was also a very kind man. So he always let the old lord win—just. How he'd have loved to play against your computer! Especially as he wrote a story about a chess-playing machine."

"He did?"

"Well, not exactly a machine; maybe an imp."

"What's it called? I must look it up."

"*The Three Sailors' Gambit*—ah, there she is! I might have guessed."

The old man's voice had softened appreciably as the little boat came into the field of view. It was drifting in lazy circles at the center of a fair-sized lake, and its sole occupant appeared to be completely engrossed in a book.

Donald Craig raised his wristcom and whispered: "Ada—we have a visitor—we'll be down in a minute." The distant figure waved a languid hand, and continued reading. Then it dwindled swiftly away as Donald zoomed the camera obscura lens.

Now Bradley could see that the lake was approximately heart-shaped, connected to a smaller, circular pond where the point of the heart should have been. That in turn opened into a third and much smaller pond, also circular. It was a curious arrangement, and obviously a recent one; the lawn still bore the scars of earth-moving machines.

"Welcome to Lake Mandelbrot," said Patrick, with noticeable lack of enthusiasm. "And be careful, Mr. Bradley—*don't* encourage her to explain it to you."

"I don't think," said Donald, "that any encouragement will be necessary. But let's go down and find out."

As her father approached with his two companions, Ada started the motor of the tiny boat; it was powered by a small solar panel, and was barely able to match their leisurely walking pace. She did not head directly toward them, as Bradley had expected, but steered the boat along the central axis of the main lake, and through the narrow isthmus connecting it to its smaller satellite. This was quickly crossed, and the boat entered the third and smallest lake of all. Though it was now only a few meters away from them, Bradley could hear no sound from its motor. His engineer's soul approved of such efficiency.

"Ada," said Donald, calling across the rapidly diminishing expanse of water. "This is the visitor I told you about—Mr. Bradley. He's going to help us raise the *Titanic*."

Ada, now preparing to enter the harbor, merely acknowledged his presence with a brief nod. The final lake—really no more than a small pond that would be overcrowded by a dozen ducks—was connected to a boathouse by a long, narrow canal.

It was perfectly straight, and Bradley realized that it lay precisely along the central axis of the three conjoined lakes. All this was obviously planned, though for what purpose he could not imagine. From the quizzical smile on Patrick's face, he guessed that the old gardener was enjoying his perplexity.

The canal was bordered on either side by beautiful cypress trees, more than twenty meters high; it was, Bradley thought, like a miniature version of the approach to the Taj Mahal. He had only seen that masterpiece briefly, years ago, but had never forgotten its splendid vista.

"You see, Pat, they're all doing fine—in spite of what you said," Donald told the head gardener.

Patrick pursed his lips and looked critically at the line of trees. He pointed to several which, to Bradley's eyes, appeared indistinguishable from the rest.

"*Those* may have to be replanted," he said. "Don't say I didn't warn you—and the Missus."

They had now reached the boathouse at the end of the tree-lined canal, and waited for Ada to complete her leisurely approach. When she was only a meter away, there was a sudden hysterical yelp and something closely resembling a small floor mop leaped out of the boat and hurled itself at Bradley's feet.

"If you don't move," said Donald, "she may decide you're harmless, and let you live."

While the tiny Cairn terrier was sniffing suspiciously at his shoes, Bradley examined her mistress. He noticed, with approval, the careful way that Ada tied up the boat, even though that was quite unnecessary; she was, he could already tell, an extremely well-organized young lady—quite a contrast to her hysterical little pet, who had switched instantly to fawning affection.

Ada scooped up Lady with one hand, and hugged the

puppy to her breast while she regarded Bradley with a look of frank curiosity.

"Are you really going to help us raise the *Titanic*?" she asked.

Bradley shifted uncomfortably and avoided returning that disconcerting stare.

"I hope so," he said evasively. "But there are lots of things we have to talk over first." And this, he added silently, is neither the time nor the place. He would have to wait until they had joined Mrs. Craig, and he was not altogether looking forward to the encounter.

"What were you reading in the boat, Ada?" he asked lightly, trying to change the subject.

"Why do you want to know?" she asked. It was a perfectly polite question, with no hint of impertinence. Bradley was still struggling for a suitable reply when Donald Craig interjected hastily: "I'm afraid my daughter hasn't much time for the social graces. She considers there are more important things in life. Like fractals and non-Euclidean geometry."

Bradley pointed to the puppy. "*That* doesn't look very geometric to me."

To his surprise, Ada rewarded him with a charming smile. "You should see Lady when she's been dried out after a bath, and her hair's pointing in all directions. Then she makes a lovely three-D fractal."

The joke was right over Bradley's head, but he joined in the general laughter. Ada had the saving grace of a sense of humor; he could get to like her—as long as he remembered to treat her as someone twice her age.

Greatly daring, he ventured another question.

"That number 1.999 painted on the boathouse," he said. "I suppose that's a reference to your mother's famous end-of-century program."

Donald Craig chuckled.

"Nice try, Jason; that's what most people guess. Let him have it gently, Ada."

The formidable Ms. Craig deposited her puppy on the grass, and it scuttled away to investigate the base of the nearest cypress. Bradley had the uncomfortable impression that Ada was trying to calibrate his I.Q. before she replied.

"If you look carefully, Mr. Bradley, you'll see there's a minus sign in front of the number, and a dot over the last nine."

"So?"

"So it's really *minus* 1.9999 . . . forever and ever."

"Amen," interjected Patrick.

"Wouldn't it have been easier to write minus two?"

"Exactly what I said," Donald said with a chuckle. "But don't tell that to a *real* mathematician."

"I thought you were a pretty good one."

"God, no—I'm just a hairy-knuckled byte-basher, compared to Edith."

"And this young lady here, I suspect. You know, I'm beginning to feel out of my depth. And in my profession, that's not a good idea."

Ada's laugh helped to lift the curious sense of unease that Bradley had felt for the last few minutes. There was something depressing about this place—something ominous that hovered just beyond the horizon of consciousness. It was no use trying to focus upon it by a deliberate act of will—the fugitive wisp of memory scuttled away as soon as he attempted to pin it down. He would have to wait; it would emerge when it was ready.

"You asked me what book I was reading, Mr. Bradley—"

"—please call me Jason—"

"—so here it is."

"I might have guessed. He was a mathematician too, wasn't

he? But I'm ashamed to say I've never read *Alice*. The nearest American equivalent is *The Wizard of Oz*."

"I've read that too, but Dodgson—Carroll—is *much* better. How he would have loved this!"

Ada waved toward the curiously shaped lakes, and the little boathouse with its enigmatic inscription.

"You see, Mr. Brad—Mr. Jason—that's the Utter West. Minus two is infinity for the M-Set—there's absolutely *nothing* beyond that. What we're walking along now is the Spike—and this little pond is the very last of the mini-sets on the negative side. One day we'll plant a border of flowers—won't we, Pat?—that will give some idea of the fantastic detail around the main lobes. And over there in the east—that cusp where the two bigger lakes meet—that's Seahorse Valley, at minus .745. The origin—zero, zero, of course—is in the middle of the biggest lake. The set doesn't extend so far to the east; the cusp at Elephant Crossing—over there, right in front of the castle—is around plus .273."

"I'll take your word for it," Bradley answered, completely overwhelmed. "You know perfectly well I haven't the faintest idea what you're talking about."

That was not perfectly true: it was obvious enough that the Craigs had used their wealth to carve this landscape into the shape of some bizarre mathematical function. It seemed a harmless enough obsession; there were many worse ways of spending money, and it must have provided a great deal of employment for the locals.

"I think that's enough, Ada," said Donald, with much more firmness than he had shown hitherto. "Let's give Mr. Jason some lunch—before we throw him head-over-heels into the M-Set."

They were leaving the tree-lined avenue, at the point where the narrow canal opened out into the smallest of the lakes, when

Bradley's brain unlocked its memory. Of course—the still expanse of water, the boat, the cypresses—all the key elements of Boecklin's painting! Incredible that he hadn't realized it before. . . .

Rachmaninoff's haunting music welled up from the depths of his mind—soothing, familiar, reassuring. Now that he had identified the cause of his faint disquiet, the shadow lifted from his spirit.

Even later, he never really believed it had been a premonition.

19.

"RAISE
THE
TITANIC!"

SLOWLY, RELUCTANTLY, THE thousands of tons of metal began to stir, like some marine monster awakening from its sleep. The explosive charges that were attempting to jolt it off the seabed blasted up great clouds of silt, which concealed the wreck in a swirling mist.

The decades-long grip of the mud began to yield; the enormous propellers lifted from the ocean floor. *Titanic* began the ascent to the world she had left, a long lifetime ago.

On the surface, the sea was already boiling from the disturbance far below. Out of the maelstrom of foam, a slender mast emerged—still carrying the crow's nest from which Frederick Fleet had once telephoned the fatal words, "Iceberg right ahead."

And now the prow came knifing up—the ruined superstructure—the whole vast expanse of decking—the giant anchors which had taken a twenty-horse team to move—the three towering funnels, and the stump of the fourth—the great cliff of steel, studded with portholes—and, at last:

TITANIC

LIVERPOOL

The monitor screen went blank; there was a momentary silence in the studio, induced by a mixture of awe, reverence, and sheer admiration for the movie's special effects.

Then Rupert Parkinson, never long at a loss for words, said ruefully: "I'm afraid it won't be quite as dramatic as that. Of course, when that movie was made, they didn't know she was in two pieces. Or that *all* the funnels had gone—though that should have been obvious."

"Is it true," asked Channel Ten's host Marcus Kilford— "Mucus" or "Killjoy" to his enemies, who were legion—"that the model they used in the movie cost more than the original ship?"

"I've heard that story—could be true, allowing for inflation."

"And the joke—"

"—that it would have been cheaper to lower the Atlantic? Believe me, I'm tired of hearing that one!"

"Then I won't mention it, of course," said Kilford, twirling the notorious monocle that was his trademark. It was widely believed that this ostentatious antique served only to hypnotize his guests, and had no optical properties whatsoever. The Physics Department of King's College, London, had even run a computer analysis of the images reflected when it caught the studio lights, and claimed to have established this with ninety-five percent certainty. The matter would only be settled when someone actually captured the thing, but all attempts had so far failed. It appeared to be immovably attached to Marcus, and he had warned would-be hijackers that it was equipped with a miniaturized self-destruct device. If this was activated, he would not be responsible for the consequences. Of course, no one believed him.

"In the film," continued Kilford, "they talked glibly about pumping foam into the hull to lift the wreck. Would that have worked?"

"Depends on how it was done. The pressure is so great— four *hundred* times atmospheric!—that all ordinary foams would collapse instantly. But we obtain essentially the same result with our microspheres—each holds its little bubble of air."

"They're strong enough to resist that enormous pressure?"

"Yes—just try and smash one!"

Parkinson scattered a handful of glass marbles across the studio coffee table. Kilford picked one up, and whistled with unfeigned surprise.

"It weighs hardly anything!"

"State of the art," Parkinson answered proudly. "And they've been tested all the way down to the bottom of the Marianas Trench—three times deeper than the *Titanic*."

Kilford turned to his other guest.

"You could have done with these on the *Mary Rose*, back in 1982—couldn't you, Dr. Thornley?"

The marine archaeologist shook her head. "Not really. That was a totally different problem. *Mary Rose* was in shallow water, and our divers were able to place a cradle under her. Then the biggest floating crane in the world pulled her up."

"It was touch and go, wasn't it?"

"Yes. A lot of people nearly had heart attacks when that metal strap gave way."

"I can believe it. Now, that hull has been sitting in South-ampton Dock for a quarter century—and it *still* isn't ready for public display. Will you do a quicker job on *Titanic*, Mr. Parkinson—assuming that you do get her up?"

"Certainly; it's the difference between wood and steel. The sea had four centuries to soak into *Mary Rose*'s timbers—no wonder it's taking decades to get it out. All the wood in *Titanic* has gone—we don't have to bother about it. Our problem is rust; and there's very little at that depth, thanks to the cold and lack of oxygen. Most of the wreck is in one of two states: excellent—or terrible."

"How many of these little . . . microspheres . . . will you need?"

"About fifty billion."

"Fifty *billion*! And how will you get them down there?"

"Very simply. We're going to *drop* them."

"With a little weight attached to each one—another fifty billion?"

Parkinson smiled, rather smugly.

"Not quite. Our Mr. Emerson has invented a technique so simple that no one believes it will work. We'll have a pipe leading down from the surface to the wreck. The water will be pumped out—and we'll simply pour the microspheres in at the top, and collect them at the bottom. They'll take only a few minutes to make the trip."

"But surely—"

"Oh, we'll have to use special air locks at both ends, but it will be essentially a continuous process. When they arrive, the microspheres will be packaged in bundles, each a cubic meter in volume. That will give a buoyancy of one ton per unit—a comfortable size for the robots to handle."

Marcus Kilford turned to the long-silent archaeologist.

"Dr. Thornley," he asked, "do you think it will work?"

"I suppose so," she said reluctantly, "but I'm not the expert on these matters. Won't that tube have to be very strong, to stand the enormous pressure at the bottom?"

"No problem; we'll use the same material. As my company's slogan says, 'You can do anything with glass'—"

"No more commercials, *please!*"

Kilford turned toward the camera, and intoned solemnly, though with a twinkle in his eye: "May I take this opportunity of denying the malicious rumor that Mr. Parkinson was spotted in a BBC cloak room, handing me a shoe box stuffed with well-used bank notes."

Everyone laughed, though behind the thick glass of the control room the producer whispered to his assistant: "If he uses that joke once again, I'll suspect it's true."

"May I ask a question?" said Dr. Thornley unexpectedly. "What about your . . . shall I say, rivals? Do you think they'll succeed first?"

"Well, let's call them friendly competitors."

"Indeed?" said Kilford skeptically. "Whoever brings their section up to the surface first will get all the publicity."

"*We're* taking the long-term view," said Parkinson. "When our grandchildren come to Florida to dive on the *Titanic*, they won't care whether we raised her up in 2012 or 2020—though of course we hope to make the centennial date." He turned to the archaeologist. "I almost wish we could use Portsmouth, and arrange for a simultaneous opening. It would be nice to have Nelson's *Victory*, Henry Eight's *Mary Rose,* and *Titanic* side by side. Four hundred years of British shipbuilding. Quite a thought."

"I'd be there," said Kilford. "But now I'd like to raise a couple of more serious matters. First of all, there's still much talk of . . . well, 'desecration' seems too strong a word, but what do you say to the people who regard *Titanic* as a tomb, and say she should be left in peace?"

"I respect their views, but it's a little late now. *Hundreds* of dives have been made on her—and on countless other ships that have gone down with great loss of life. People only seem to raise objections to *Titanic*! How many people died in *Mary Rose*, Dr. Thornley? And has anyone protested about your work?"

"About six hundred—almost half as many casualties as *Titanic*—and for a ship a fraction of the size! No—we've never had any serious complaints; in fact the whole country approved of the operation. After all, it was mostly supported by private funds."

"Another point which isn't widely realized," added Parkinson: "Very few people could have actually died *in* the *Titanic;* most of them got off, and were drowned or frozen."

"No chance of bodies?"

"None whatsoever. There are lots of very hungry creatures down there."

"Well, I'm glad we've disposed of that depressing subject. But there's something perhaps more important. . . ." Kilford picked up one of the little glass spheres, and rolled it between thumb and forefinger. "You're putting *billions* of these in the sea. Inevitably, lots of them will be lost. What about the ecological impact?"

"I see you've been reading the Bluepeace literature. Well, there won't be any."

"Not even when they wash to shore—and our beaches are littered with broken glass?"

"I'd like to shoot the copywriter who coined that phrase—or hire him. First of all, it will take *centuries*—maybe millennia—for these spheres to disintegrate. And please remember what they're made of—*silica*! So when they do eventually crumble, do you realize what they'll turn into? That well-known beach pollutant—sand!"

"Good point. But what about the other objection? Suppose fish or marine animals eat them?"

Parkinson picked up one of the microspheres, and twirled it between his fingers just as Kilford had done.

"Glass is totally nonpoisonous—chemically inert. Anything big enough to swallow one of these won't be hurt by it."

And he popped the sphere into his mouth.

Behind the control panel, the producer turned to Roy Emerson.

"That was terrific—but I'm still sorry you wouldn't go on."

"Parky did very well without me. Do you think I'd have gotten in any more words than poor Dr. Thornley?"

"Probably not. And that was a neat trick, swallowing the microsphere—don't think I could manage it. And I'll make a bet that from now on, everyone's going to call them Parky's Pills."

Emerson laughed. "I wouldn't be surprised. And he'll be asked to repeat the act, every time he goes on TV."

He thought it unnecessary to add that, besides his many other talents, Parkinson was quite a good amateur conjurer. Even with freeze-frame, no one would be able to spot what had *really* happened to that pill.

And there was another reason why he preferred not to join the panel—he was an outsider, and this was a family affair.

Though they lay centuries apart, *Mary Rose* and *Titanic* had much in common. Both were spectacular triumphs of British shipbuilding genius—sunk by equally spectacular examples of British incompetence.

20.
INTO THE
M-SET

IT WAS HARD TO BELIEVE, Jason Bradley told himself, that people actually *lived* like this, only a few generations ago. Though Conroy Castle was a very modest example of its species, its scale was still impressive to anyone who had spent most of his life in cluttered offices, motel rooms, ships' cabins—not to mention deep-diving minisubs, so cramped that the personal hygiene of your companions was a matter of crucial importance.

The dining room, with its ornately carved ceiling and enormous wall mirrors, could comfortably seat at least fifty people. Donald Craig felt it necessary to explain the little four-place table that looked lost and lonely at its center.

"We've not had time to buy proper furniture. The castle's own stuff was in terrible shape—most of it had to be burned. And we've been too busy to do much entertaining. But one day, when we've finally established ourselves as the local nobility . . ."

Edith did not seem to approve of her husband's flippancy, and once again Bradley had the impression that she was the leader in this enterprise, with Donald a reluctant—or at best passive—accomplice. He could guess the scenario: people with enough money to squander on expensive toys often discovered that they would have been happier without them. And Conroy Castle—with all its surrounding acres and maintenance staff—must be a very expensive toy indeed.

When the servants (servants!—that was another novelty) had cleared the remnants of an excellent Chinese dinner flown in especially from Dublin, Bradley and his hosts retreated to a set of comfortable armchairs in the adjoining room.

"We won't let you get away," said Donald, "without giving you our Child's Guide to the M-Set. Edith can spot a Mandel-virgin at a hundred meters."

Bradley was not sure if he qualified for this description. He had finally recognized the odd shape of the lake, though he had forgotten its technical name until reminded of it. In the last decade of the century, it had been impossible to escape from manifestations of the Mandelbrot Set—they were appearing all the time on video displays, wallpaper, fabrics, and virtually every type of design. Bradley recalled that someone had coined the word "Mandelmania" to describe the more acute symptoms; he had begun to suspect that it might be applicable to this odd household. But he was quite prepared to sit with polite interest through whatever lecture or demonstration his hosts had in store for him.

He realized that they too were being polite, in their own way. They were anxious to have his decision, and he was equally anxious to give it.

He only hoped that the call he was expecting would come through before he left the castle. . . .

Bradley had never met the traditional stage mother, but he had seen her in movies like—what was that old one called?—ah, *Fame*. Here was the same passionate determination on the part of a parent for a child to become a star, even if there was no discernible talent. In this case, he did not doubt that the faith was fully justified.

"Before Ada begins," said Edith, "I'd like to make a few points. The M-Set is the most complex entity in the whole of mathematics—yet it doesn't involve anything more advanced than addition and multiplication—not even subtraction or division! That's why many people with a good knowledge of math have difficulty in grasping it. They simply can't believe that something with too much detail to be explored before the end of the Universe can be generated without using logs or trig functions or higher transcendentals. It doesn't seem reasonable that it's all done merely by adding numbers together."

"Doesn't seem reasonable to me, either. If it's so simple, why didn't anyone discover it centuries ago?"

"Very good question! Because so much adding and multiplying is involved, with such huge numbers, that we had to wait for high-speed computers. If you'd given abacuses to Adam and Eve and *all* their descendants right up to now, they couldn't have found some of the pictures Ada can show you by pressing a few keys. Go ahead, dear. . . ."

The holoprojector was cunningly concealed; Bradley could not even guess where it was hiding. Very easy to make this old castle a haunted one, he thought, and scare away any intruders. It would beat a burglar alarm.

The two crossed lines of an ordinary x-y diagram appeared in the air, with the sequence of integers 0, 1, 2, 3, 4 . . . marching off in all four directions.

Ada gave Bradley that disconcertingly direct look, as if she were once again trying to estimate his I.Q. so that her presentation could be appropriately calibrated.

"Any point on this plane," she said, "can be identified by two numbers—its x- and y-coordinates. Okay?"

"Okay," Bradley answered solemnly.

"Well, the M-Set lies in a very small region near the origin—it doesn't extend beyond plus or minus two in either direction, so we can ignore all the larger numbers."

The integers skittered off along the four axes, leaving only the numbers one and two marking distances away from the central zero.

"Now suppose we take any point inside this grid, and join it to the center. Measure the length of this radius—let's call it r."

This, thought Bradley, is putting no great strain on my mental resources. When do we get to the tricky part?

"Obviously, in this case r can have any value from zero to just under three—about two point eight, to be exact. Okay?"

"Okay."

"Right. Now Exercise One. Take any point's r value, and square it. *Keep on squaring it*. What happens?"

"Don't let me spoil your fun, Ada."

"Well, if r is exactly one, it stays at that value—no matter how many times you square it. One times one times one times one is always one."

"Okay," said Bradley, just beating Ada to the draw.

"If it's even a *smidgin* more than one, however, and you go on squaring it, sooner or later it will shoot off to infinity. Even if it's 1.0000 . . . 0001, and there are a million zeros to the right of the decimal point. It will just take a bit longer.

"But if the number is *less* than one—say .99999999 . . . with a million nines—you get just the opposite. It may stay close to one for ages, but as you keep on squaring it, suddenly it will collapse and dwindle away down to zero—okay?"

This time Ada got there first, and Bradley merely nodded. As yet, he could not see the point in this elementary arithmetic, but it was obviously leading somewhere.

"Lady—stop bothering Mr. Bradley! So you see, simply squaring numbers—and going on squaring them, over and over—divides them into two distinct sets. . . ."

A circle had appeared on the two crossed axes, centered on the origin and with radius unity.

"Inside that circle are all the numbers that disappear when you keep on squaring them. Outside are all those that shoot off to infinity. You could say that the circle of radius one is a fence—a boundary—a *frontier*—dividing the two sets of numbers. I like to call it the S-set."

"S for squaring?"

"Of cour— Yes. Now, here's the important point. The numbers on either side are totally separated; yet though nothing can pass through it, the boundary hasn't any thickness. It's simply a line—you could go on magnifying it forever and it would stay a line, though it would soon appear to be a straight one because you wouldn't be able to see its curvature."

"This may not seem very exciting," interjected Donald, "but it's absolutely fundamental—you'll soon see why—sorry, Ada."

"Now, to get the M-Set we make one teeny-*weeny* change. We don't just square the numbers. We square and *add* . . . square and *add*. You wouldn't think it would make all that difference—but it opens up a whole new universe. . . .

"Suppose we start with one again. We square it and get one. Then we add them to get two.

"Two squared is four. Add the original one again—answer five.

"Five squared is twenty-five—add one—twenty-six.

"Twenty-six squared is six hundred seventy-six—you see what's happening! The numbers are shooting up at a fantastic rate. A few more times around the loop, and they're too big for any computer to handle. Yet we started with—*one*! So that's the *first* big difference between the M-Set and the S-set, which has its boundary at one.

"But if we started with a much smaller number than one—say zero point one—you'll probably guess what happens."

"It collapses to nothing after a few cycles of squaring and adding."

Ada gave her rare but dazzling smile.

"*Usually.* Sometimes it dithers around a small, fixed value—anyway, it's trapped inside the set. So once again we have a map that divides all the numbers on the plane into two classes. Only this time, the boundary isn't something as elementary as a circle."

"You can say that again," murmured Donald. He collected a frown from Edith, but pressed on. "I've asked quite a few people what shape they thought would be produced; most suggested some kind of oval. No one came near the truth; no one ever could. All *right*, Lady! I won't interrupt Ada again!"

"Here's the first approximation," continued Ada, scooping up her boisterous puppy with one hand while tapping the keyboard with the other. "You've already seen it today."

The now-familiar outline of Lake Mandelbrot had appeared superimposed on the grid of unit squares, but in far more detail than Bradley had seen it in the garden. On the right was the largest, roughly heart-shaped figure, then a smaller circle touching it, a much smaller one touching *that*—and the narrow spike running off to the extreme left and ending at—2 on the x-axis.

Now, however, Bradley could see that the main figures were barnacled—that was the metaphor that came instantly to mind—with a myriad of smaller subsidiary circles, many of which had short jagged lines extending from them. It was a much more complex shape than the pattern of lakes in the garden—strange and intriguing, but certainly not at all beautiful. Edith and Ada, however, were looking at it with a kind of reverential awe, which Donald did not seem to entirely share.

"This is the complete set with no magnification," said Ada, in a voice that was now a little less self-assured—in fact, almost hushed.

"Even on this scale, though, you can see how different it is from the plain, zero-thickness circle bounding the S-set. You could zoom *that* up forever and ever, and it would remain a line—nothing more. But the boundary of the M-Set is *fuzzy*—it contains infinite detail: you can go in anywhere you like, and magnify as much as you please—and you'll always discover something new and unexpected—look!"

The image expanded; they were diving into the cleft between the main cardioid and its tangent circle. It was, Bradley told himself, very much like watching a zip-fastener being pulled open—except that the teeth of the zipper had the most extraordinary shapes.

First they looked like baby elephants, waving tiny trunks. Then the trunks became tentacles. Then the tentacles sprouted eyes. Then, as the image continued to expand, the eyes opened up into black whirlpools of infinite depth. . . .

"The magnification's up in the millions now," Edith whispered. "The picture we started with is already bigger than Europe."

They swept past the whirlpools, skirting mysterious islands guarded by reefs of coral. Flotillas of seahorses sailed by in stately procession. At the screen's exact center, a tiny black dot appeared, expanded, began to show a haunting familiarity—and seconds later revealed itself as an exact replica of the original set.

This, Bradley thought, is where we came in. Or is it? He could not be quite sure; there seemed to be minor differences, but the family resemblance was unmistakable.

"Now," continued Ada, "our original picture is as wide as

the orbit of Mars—so this mini-set's really far smaller than an atom. But there's just as much detail all around it. And so on forever."

The zooming stopped; for a moment it seemed that a sample of lacework, full of intricate loops and whorls that teased the eye, hung frozen in space. Then, as if a paintbox had been spilled over it, the monochrome image burst into colors so unexpected, and so dazzlingly beautiful, that Bradley gave a gasp of astonishment.

The zooming restarted, but in the reverse direction, and in a micro-universe now transformed by color. No one said a word until they were back at the original complete M-Set, now an ominous black fringed with a narrow border of golden fire, and shooting off jagged lightnings of blues and purples.

"And where," asked Bradley when he had recovered his breath, "did all those colors come from? We didn't see them on the way in."

Ada laughed. "No—they're not really part of the set—but aren't they gorgeous? I can tell the computer to make them anything I like."

"Even though the actual colors are quite arbitrary," Edith explained, "they're full of meaning. You know the way map makers put shades of blue and green between contour lines, to emphasize differences in level?"

"Of course; we do just the same thing in oceanography. The deeper the blue, the deeper the water."

"Right. In this case, the colors tell us how many times the computer's had to go around the loop before it decides whether a number definitely belongs to the M-Set—or not. In borderline cases, it may have to do the squaring and adding routine thousands of times."

"And often for hundred-digit numbers," said Donald. "*Now* you understand why the set wasn't discovered earlier."

"Mighty good reason."

"Now watch this," said Ada.

The image came to life as waves of color flowed outward. It seemed that the borders of the set itself were continually expanding—yet staying in the same place. Then Bradley realized that nothing was really moving; only the colors were cycling around the spectrum, to produce this completely convincing illusion of movement.

I begin to understand, Bradley thought, how someone could get lost in this thing—even make it a way of life.

"I'm almost certain," he said, "that I've seen this program listed in my computer's software library—with a couple of thousand others. How lucky I've never run it. I can see how addictive it could get."

He noticed that Donald Craig glanced sharply at Edith, and realized that he had made a somewhat tactless remark. However, she still seemed engrossed by the flow of colors, even though she must have seen this particular display countless times.

"Ada," she said dreamily, "give Mr. Jason our favorite quotation from Einstein."

That's asking a lot from a ten-year-old, thought Bradley—even one like this; but the girl never hesitated, and there was no trace of mechanical repetition in her voice. She understood the words, and spoke from the heart:

" 'The most beautiful thing we can experience is the mysterious. It is the source of all true art and science. He to whom this emotion is a stranger, who can no longer pause to wonder and stand wrapt in awe, is as good as dead.' "

I'll go along with that, thought Bradley. He remembered calm nights in the Pacific, with a skyfull of stars and a glimmering trail of bioluminescence behind the ship; he recalled his first glimpse of the teeming life-forms—as alien as any from another planet—gathered around the scalding cornucopia of a Galápagos mid-ocean vent, where the continents were slowly tearing apart; and he hoped that before long he would feel awe and wonder again, when the tremendous knife edge of *Titanic*'s prow came looming up out of the abyss.

The dance of colors ceased: the M-Set faded out. Although nothing had ever been *really* there, he could somehow sense that the virtual screen of the holograph projector had switched off.

"So now," said Donald, "you know more about the Mandelbrot Set than you want to." He glanced momentarily at Edith, and once again Bradley felt that twinge of sympathy toward him.

It was not at all the feeling he had expected, when he came to Conroy Castle; "envy" would have been a better word. Here was a man with great wealth, a beautiful home, and a talented and attractive family—all the ingredients which were supposed to guarantee happiness. Yet something had obviously gone wrong. I wonder, Bradley thought, how long it is since they went to bed together. It could be as simple as that—though *that*, of course, was seldom simple. . . .

Once again he glanced at his watch; they must think he was deliberately avoiding the issue—and they were perfectly right. Hurry up, Mr. Director-General! he pleaded silently.

As if on cue, he felt the familiar tingling in his wrist.

"Excuse me," he said to his hosts. "I've a very important call coming through. It will only take a minute."

"Of course. We'll leave you to it."

How many million times a day this ritual was now carried out! Strict etiquette dictated that everyone else offer to leave the room when a personal call was coming through; politeness demanded that only the recipient leave, with apologies to all. There were countless variations according to circumstances and nationalities. In Japan, so Kato was fond of complaining, the formalities often lasted so long that the caller hung up in disgust.

"Sorry for the interruption," Bradley said as he came back in through the French windows. "That was about our business—I couldn't give you a decision until I'd received it."

"I hope it's a favorable one," said Donald. "We need you."

"And I would like to work with you—but—"

"Parky's made you a better offer," said Edith, with scarcely veiled contempt.

Bradley looked at her calmly, and answered without rancor.

"No, Mrs. Craig. Please keep these figures confidential. The Parkinson group's offer was generous—but it was only half of yours. And the offer which I've just received is much less than one tenth of *that*. Nevertheless, I'm considering it very seriously."

There was a resounding silence, broken at last by an uncharacteristic giggle from Ada.

"You must be crazy," said Edith. Donald merely grinned.

"You may be right. But I've reached the stage when I don't need the money, though it's always good to have some around." He paused, and chuckled softly.

"Enough is enough. I don't know if you ever heard the wisecrack that *Titanic*'s most famous casualty, J. J. Astor, once made: "A man who has a million dollars is as well off as one who is rich." Well, I've made a few million during my career, and some of it's still in the bank. I don't really need any more; and if I do, I can always go down and tickle another octopus.

"I didn't *plan* this—it was a bolt from the blue—two days ago I'd already decided to accept your offer."

Edith now seemed more perplexed than hostile.

"Can you tell us who's . . . *underbid* Nippon-Turner?"

Bradley shook his head. "Give me a couple of days; there

are still a few problems, and I don't want to fall between *three* stools."

"I think I understand," said Donald. "There's only one reason to work for peanuts. Every man owes something to his profession."

"That sounds like a quotation."

"It is: Dr. Johnson."

"I like it; I may be using it a lot, in the next few weeks. Meanwhile, before I make a final decision, I want a little time to think matters over. Again, many thanks for your hospitality— not to mention your offer. I may yet accept it—but if not, I hope we can still be friends."

As he lifted away from the castle, the downwash of the helicopter ruffled the waters of Lake Mandelbrot, shattering the reflections of the cypresses. He was contemplating the biggest break in his career; before he made his decision, he needed to relax completely.

And he knew exactly how to do that.

21.
A HOUSE
OF GOOD
REPUTE

EVEN THE COMING of hypersonic transportation had not done much to change the status of New Zealand; to most people it was merely the last stop before the South Pole. The great majority of New Zealanders were quite content to keep it that way.

Evelyn Merrick was one of the exceptions, and had defected at the (in her case, very) ripe age of seventeen to find her destiny elsewhere. After three marriages which had left her emotionally scarred but financially secure, she had discovered her role in life, and was as happy as anyone could reasonably expect to be.

The Villa, as it was known to her wide-ranging clientele, was on a beautiful estate in one of the still unspoiled parts of Kent, conveniently close to Gatwick Airport. Its previous owner had been a celebrated media tycoon, who had placed his bet on the wrong system when high-definition TV swept all before it at the end of the Twentieth Century. Later attempts to restore his fortune had misfired, and he was now a guest of His Majesty's government for the next five years (assuming time off for good behavior).

Being a man of high moral standards, he was quite indignant about the use which Dame Eva had now made of his property, and had even attempted to dislodge her. However, Eva's lawyers were just as good as his; perhaps better, since she was still at liberty, and had every intention of remaining so.

The Villa was run with meticulous propriety, the girls' passports, tax returns, health and pension contributions, medical records, and so forth being instantly available to any government inspector—of whom, Dame Eva sometimes remarked sourly, there always seemed to be a copious supply. If any ever came in the hope of personal gratification, they were sadly disappointed.

On the whole, it was a rewarding career, full of emotional and intellectual stimulus. She certainly had no ethical problems, having long ago decided that anything enjoyed by adults of voting age was perfectly acceptable, as long as it was not dangerous, unhygienic, or fattening. Her main cause of complaint was that involvement with clients caused a high rate of staff turnover, with resulting heavy expenditure on wedding presents. She had also observed that Villa-inspired marriages appeared to last longer than those with more conventional origins, and intended to publish a statistical survey when she was quite sure of her data; at the moment the correlation coefficient was still below the level of significance.

As might be expected in her profession, Evelyn Merrick was a woman of many secrets, mostly other peoples'; but she also had one of her own which she guarded with special care. Though nothing could have been more respectable, if it came out it might be bad for trade. For the last two years, she had been employing her extensive—perhaps unique—knowledge of paraphilia to complete her doctor's degree in psychology at the University of Auckland.

She had never met Professor Hinton, except over video circuits—and even that very rarely, since both preferred the digital impersonality of computer file exchanges. One day—perhaps a decade after she had retired—her thesis would be published, though not under her own name, and with all the case histories disguised beyond identification. Not even Professor Hinton knew the individuals involved, though he had made some shrewd guesses at a few.

"Subject O.G.," Eva typed. "Age fifty. Successful engineer."

She considered the screen carefully. The initials, of course, had been changed according to her simple code, and the age had been rounded down to the nearest decade. But the last entry was reasonably accurate: his profession reflected a man's personality, and should not be disguised unless it was absolutely necessary to avoid identification. Even then, it had to be done with sensitivity, so that the displacement was not too violent. In the case of a world-famous musician, Eva had altered "pianist" to "violinist," and she had converted an equally celebrated sculptor into a painter. She had even turned a politician into a statesman.

". . . As a small boy, O.G. was teased and occasionally captured by the pupils of a neighboring girl's school, who used him as a (fairly willing) subject for lessons in nursing and male anatomy. They frequently bandaged him from head to foot, and though he now asserts that there was no erotic element involved, this is rather hard to believe. When challenged, he shrugs his shoulders and says, 'I just don't remember.'

"Later, as a young man, O.G. witnessed the aftermath of a major accident which caused many deaths. Though not injured himself, the experience also appears to have affected his sexual fantasies. He enjoys various forms of bondage (see List A) and he had developed a mild case of the Saint Sebastian Complex, most famously demonstrated by Yukio Mishima. Unlike Mishima, however, O.G. is completely heterosexual, scoring only 2.5 +/- 0.1 on the Standard Mapplethorpe Phototest.

"What makes O.G.'s behavior pattern so interesting, and perhaps unusual, is that he is an active and indeed somewhat aggressive personality, as befits the manager of an organization in a demanding and competitive business. It is hard to imagine him playing a *passive* role in any sphere of life, yet he likes my personnel to wrap him up in bandages like an Egyptian mummy, until he is completely helpless. Only in this way, after considerable stimulation, can he achieve a satisfactory orgasm.

"When I suggested that he was acting out a death wish, he laughed but did not attempt to deny it. His work often involves physical danger, which may be the very reason why he was attracted to it in the first place. However, he gave an alternative explanation which, I am sure, contains a good deal of truth.

" 'When you have responsibilities involving millions of dollars and affecting many men's lives, you can't imagine how delightful it is to be *completely* helpless for a while—unable to control what's happening around you. Of course, I *know* it's all play-acting, but I manage to pretend it isn't. I sometimes wonder how I'd enjoy the situation if it was for real.'

" 'You wouldn't,' I told him, and he agreed."

Eva scrolled the entry, checking it for any clues that might reveal O.G.'s identity. The Villa specialized in celebrities, so it was better to be excessively cautious than the reverse.

That caution extended to the celebrities themselves. The Villa's only house rule was "No blood on the carpets," and she recalled, with a grimace of disgust, a third world country's chief-of-staff whose frenzies had injured one of her girls. Eva had accepted his apologies, and his check, with cold disdain, then made a quick call to the Foreign Office. The general would have been most surprised—and mortified—to know exactly why the British ambassador now found so many reasons for postponing his next visit to the United Kingdom.

Eva sometimes wondered what dear Sister Margarita would have thought of her star pupil's present vocation; the last time she had wept was when the notice of her old friend's death had reached her from the Mother Superior. And she remembered, with wistful amusement, the question she had once been tempted to ask her tutor: exactly *why* should a vow of perpetual chastity be considered any nobler—any *holier*—than a vow of perpetual constipation?

It was a perfectly serious query, not in the least intended to scandalize the old nun or shake the sure foundations of her faith. But on the whole, perhaps it was just as well left unasked.

Sister Margarita already knew that little Eva Merrick was not meant for the church; but Eva still sent a generous donation to St. Jude's every Christmas.

22.
BUREAUCRAT

Article 156
Establishment of the Authority

1. There is hereby established the International Seabed Authority, which shall function in accordance with this Part.

2. All States Parties are *ipso facto* members of the Authority.

. . . . .

4. The seat of the Authority shall be in Jamaica.

Article 158
Organs of the Authority

2. There is hereby established the Enterprise, the organ through which the Authority shall carry out the functions referred to in article 170, paragraph 1.

(United Nations Convention on the Law of the Sea, signed at Montego Bay, Jamaica, on 10 December 1982.)

"SORRY ABOUT the emoluments," said Director-General Wilbur Jantz apologetically, "but they're fixed by U.N. regulations."

"I quite understand. As you know, I'm not here for the money."

"And there *are* very considerable fringe benefits. First, you'll have the rank of ambassador . . ."

"Will I have to dress like one? I hope not—I don't even have a tux, let alone the rest of that damned nonsense."

Jantz laughed.

"Don't worry—we'll take care of details like that. And you'll be VIPed everywhere, of course—that can be quite pleasant."

It's a long time, thought Jason Bradley, since I've *not* been VIPed, but it would be rather tactless to say so. Despite all his experience, he was a new boy in this environment; maybe he shouldn't have made that crack about ambassadors. . . .

The D.G. was scanning the readout scrolling on his desk display, giving an occasional PAUSE command so that he could examine some item in detail. Bradley would have returned a substantial slice of his income to his new employers for the privilege of reading that file. I wonder if they know, he thought, about the time that Ted and I "salted" that wreck off Delos with fake amphorae? Not that I've got a guilty conscience: it caused a lot of trouble to people who thoroughly deserved it.

"I think I should tell you," said the D.G., "that we did have one small problem—though I shouldn't worry about it. Some of our more, ah, aggressively independent states-parties may not be too happy about your CIA connection."

"That was more than thirty years ago! And I didn't even know it was a CIA job until long after I'd signed up—as an ordinary seaman, for heaven's sake. . . . I thought I was joining Hughes' Summa Corporation—and so I was."

"Don't let it lose you any sleep; I mention it just in case someone brings it up. It's not likely, because in all other respects your qualifications are superb. Even Ballard admitted that."

"Oh—he did?"

"Well, he said you were the best of a bad bunch."

"That sounds like Bob."

The D.G. continued to examine the readout, then sat for a moment with a thoughtful expression.

"This has nothing to do with your appointment, and please excuse me if I'm speaking out of turn. I'm talking to you as man to man—"

Hello, thought Jason, they know about the Villa! I wonder how they got through Eva's security?

But it was a much bigger surprise than *that*. . . .

"It seems that you lost contact with your son and his mother more than twenty years ago. If you wish, we can put you in touch."

For a moment, Bradley felt a constriction in his chest; it was almost as if something had happened to his air supply. He knew the sensation all too well, and felt the clammy onset of that disabling panic which is a diver's worst enemy.

As he had always managed to do before, he regained control by slow, deep breathing. Director-General Jantz, realizing that he had opened some old wound, waited sympathetically.

"Thank you," Bradley said at last. "I would prefer not to. Are they . . . all right?"

"Yes."

That was all he needed to know. It was impossible to turn back the clock: he could barely remember the man—*boy!*—he had been at twenty-five, when he had finally gone to college. And, for the first and last time, fallen in love.

He would never know whose fault it was, and perhaps now it did not matter. They could have contacted him easily enough, if they had wished. (Did JJ ever think of him, and recall the times they had played together? Bradley's eyes stung, and he turned his mind away from the memory.)

He sometimes wondered if he would even recognize Julie if they met in the street; as he had destroyed all her photographs (why had he kept that one of J.J.?), he could no longer clearly remember her face. There was no doubt, however, that the experience had left indelible scars on his psyche, but he had learned to live with them—with the help, he wryly admitted, of Dame Eva. The ritual he had institutionalized at the Villa had brought him mental and physical relief, and had allowed him to function efficiently. He was grateful for that.

And now he had a new interest—a new challenge—as deputy director (Atlantic) of the International Seabed Authority. He could just imagine how Ted Collier would have laughed his head off at this metamorphosis. Well, there was much truth in the old saying that poachers made the best gamekeepers.

"I've asked Dr. Zwicker to come and say hello, as you'll be working closely together. Have you ever met him before?"

"No—but of course I've seen him often enough. Last time was only yesterday, on the Science News Channel. He was analyzing the Parkinson scheme—and didn't think much of it."

"Between you and me, he doesn't think much of anything he hasn't invented himself. And he's usually right, which doesn't endear him to his colleagues."

Most people still thought it slightly comic that the world's leading oceanographer had been born in an alpine valley, and there had been endless jokes about the prowess of the Swiss Navy. But there was no getting away from the fact that the bathyscaphe had been invented in Switzerland, and the long shadow of the Piccards still lay across the technology they had founded.

The director-general glanced at his watch, and smiled at Bradley.

"If my conscience would allow it, I could win bets this way." He started a quiet countdown, and had just reached "One" when there was a knock on the door.

"See what I mean?" he said to Bradley. "As they're so fond of saying, 'Time is the art of the Swiss.'" Then he called out: "Come in, Franz."

There was a moment of silent appraisal before scientist and engineer shook hands; each knew the other's reputation, and each was wondering, "Will we be colleagues—or antagonists?" Then Professor Franz Zwicker said, "Welcome aboard, Mr. Bradley. We have much to talk about."

PREPARATIONS

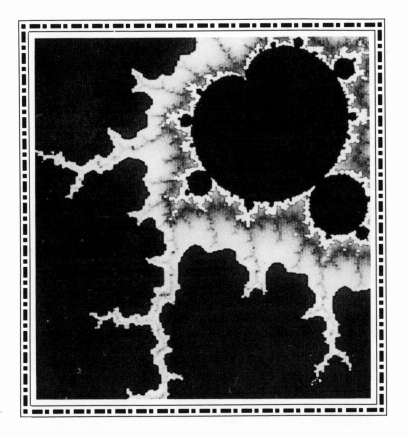

23.

PHONE-IN

"THERE CAN'T BE many people," said Marcus Kilford, "who don't know that it's now less than four years to the *Titanic* centennial—or haven't heard about the plans to raise the wreck. Once again, I'm happy to have with me three of the leaders in this project. I'll talk to each of them in turn—then you'll have a chance of calling in with any specific questions you have. At the right time, the number will flash along the bottom of the screen. . . .

"The gentleman on my left is the famous underwater engineer Jason Bradley; his encounter with the giant octopus in the Newfoundland oil rig is now part of ocean folklore. He's currently with the International Seabed Authority, and is responsible for monitoring operations on the wreck.

"Next to him is Rupert Parkinson, who *almost* brought the America's Cup to England last year. (Sorry about that, Rupert.) His firm is involved in raising the forward portion of the wreck—the larger of the two pieces into which the ship is broken.

"On my right is Donald Craig, who's associated with the Nippon-Turner Corporation—now the world's largest media chain. He will tell us about the plans to raise the stern, which was the last part to sink—carrying with it most of those who were lost on that unforgettable night, ninety-six years ago. . . .

"Mr. Bradley—would it be fair to call you a referee, making sure that there's no cheating in the race between these two gentlemen?"

Kilford had to hold up his hand to quell simultaneous protests from his other two guests.

"Please, gentlemen! You'll both have your turn. Let Jason speak first."

Now that I'm disguised as a diplomat, thought Bradley, I'd better try to act the part. I know Kilford's trying to needle us—that's his job—so I'll play it cool.

"I don't regard it as a *race*," he answered carefully. "Both parties have submitted schedules which call for the raising mid-April 2012."

"On the fifteenth itself? *Both* of them?"

This was a sensitive matter, which Bradley had no intention of discussing in public. He had convinced ISA's top brass that nothing like a photo finish must be allowed. Two major salvage operations could not possibly take place *simultaneously*, less than a kilometer apart. The risk of disaster—always a major concern—could be greatly increased. Trying to perform two difficult jobs at once was a very good recipe for achieving neither.

"Look," he said patiently, "this isn't a one-day operation. *Titanic* reached the bottom in a matter of minutes. It's going to take days to lift her back to the surface. Perhaps weeks."

"May I make a point?" said Parkinson, promptly doing so. "We have no intention of bringing our section of the wreck *back to the surface*. It's always going to remain completely underwater, to avoid the risk of immediate corrosion. *We're* not engaged in a TV spectacular." He carefully avoided looking at Craig; the studio camera was less diffident.

I feel sorry for Donald, thought Bradley. Kato should have been here instead: he and Parky would be well matched. We might see some real fireworks, as each tried to be more sardonically polite than the other—in, of course, the most gentlemanly way possible. Bradley wished that he could help Donald, toward whom he had developed a warm, almost paternal feeling, but he had to remember that he was now a friendly neutral.

Donald Craig wriggled uncomfortably in his chair, and gave Parkinson a hurt look. Kilford seemed to be enjoying himself.

"Well, Mr. Craig? Aren't you hoping to film the stern rising out of the water, with your synthetic iceberg looming over it?"

That was exactly what Kato intended, though he had never said so in public. But this was not the sort of secret that could be kept for more than a few milliseconds in the electronic global village.

"Well—er," began Donald lamely. "If we *do* bring our section up above sea level, it won't be there for long—"

"—but long enough for some spectacular footage?"

"—because just as you intend to do, Rupert, we'll tow it underwater until it reaches its final resting place, at Tokyo-on-Sea. And there's no danger of corrosion; most of the ironwork will still be enclosed in ice, and all of it will be at freezing point."

Donald paused for a second; then a slow smile spread over his face.

"And by the way," he continued, obviously gaining confidence, "haven't I heard that *you* are planning a TV spectacular? What's this story about taking scuba divers down to the wreck, as soon as it's within reach? How deep will that be, Mr. Bradley?"

"Depends what they're breathing. Thirty meters with air. A hundred or more with mixtures."

"Then I'm sure half the sports divers in the world would love to pay a visit—long before you get to Florida."

"Thanks for the suggestion, Donald," said Parkinson amiably. "We'll certainly give it a thought."

"Well, now we've broken the ice—ha, ha!—let's get down to business. What I'd like you to do—Donald, Rupert—is for each of you to explain where your project stands at the moment. I don't expect you to give away any secrets, of course. Then I'll ask Jason to make any comments—if he wants to. As C comes before P, you go on first, Donald."

"Well—um—the problem with the stern is that it's so badly smashed up. Sealing it in ice is the most sensible way of handling it as a single unit. And, of course, ice *floats*—as Captain Smith apparently forgot in 1912.

"My friends in Japan have worked out a very efficient method of freezing water, using electric current. It's already at almost zero centigrade down there, so very little additional cooling is needed.

"We've manufactured the neutral-buoyancy cables and the thermoelectric elements, and our underwater robots will start installing them in a few days. We're still negotiating for the electricity, and hope to have contracts signed very soon."

"And when you've made your deep-sea iceberg, what then?"

"Ah—well—that's something I'd rather not discuss at the moment."

Though none of those present knew it, Donald was not stalling. He was genuinely ignorant—even baffled. What *had* Kato meant in their last conversation? Surely he must have been joking: really, it was not very polite to leave his partners in the dark. . . .

"Very well, Donald. Any comments, Jason?"

Bradley shook his head. "Nothing important. The scheme's audacious, but our scientists can't fault it. And, of course, it has—what do you say?—poetic justice."

"Rupert?"

"I agree. It's a lovely idea. I only *hope* it works."

Parkinson managed to convey a genuine sense of regret for the failure he obviously expected. It was a masterly little performance.

"Well, it's your turn. Where do you stand?"

"We're using straightforward techniques—nothing exotic! Because air is compressed four hundred times at *Titanic's* depth, it's not practical to pump it down to get lift. So we're using hollow glass spheres; they have the same buoyancy at any depth. They'll be packed—millions of them—in bundles of the appropriate size. Some may be put in the ship at strategic points, by small ROVs—sorry, Remote Operated Vehicles. But most of them will be attached to a lifting cradle we're lowering down to the hull."

"And just how," interjected Kilford, "are you going to attach the *hull* to the *cradle*?"

Kilford had obviously done his homework, Bradley thought admiringly. Most laymen would have taken such a matter for granted, as a point not worth special attention; but it was the key to the whole operation.

Rupert Parkinson smiled broadly. "Donald has his little secrets; so have we. But we'll be doing some tests very shortly, and Jason has kindly agreed to observe them—haven't you?"

"Yes—if the U.S. Navy can lend us *Marvin* in time. ISA doesn't have any deep subs of its own, alas. But we're working on it."

"One day I'd like to dive with you—I think," said Kilford. "Can you get a video link down to the wreck?"

"No problem, with fiber optics. We have several monitoring circuits already."

"Splendid. I'll start bullying my producer. Well, I see there are lots of lights flashing. Our first caller is Mr.—sorry, I guess that's Miss—Chandrika de Silva of Notting Hill Gate. Go ahead, Chandrika. . . ."

24.
ICE

"WE'RE IN A BUYER'S market," said Kato with undisguised glee. "The U.S. and USSR navies are trying to underbid each other. If we got tough, I think they'd both *pay* us to take their radioactive toys off their hands."

On the other side of the world, the Craigs were watching him through the latest marvel of communications technology. POLAR 1, opened with great fanfare only a few weeks ago, was the first fiber-optic cable to be laid under the Arctic ice cap. By eliminating the long haul up to the geostationary orbit, and its slight but annoying time delay, the global phone system had been noticeably improved; speakers no longer kept interrupting each other, or wasting time waiting for replies. As the Director-General of INTELSAT had said, smiling bravely through his tears, "Now we can devote comsats to the job God intended them for—providing service to airplanes and ships and automobiles—and *everyone* who likes to get out into the fresh air."

"Have you made a deal yet?" asked Donald.

"It will be wrapped up by the end of the week. One Russki, one Yank. Then they'll compete to see which will do the better job for us. Isn't that nicer than throwing nukes at each other?"

"Much nicer."

"The British and French are also trying to get into the act—that helps our bargaining position, of course. We may even rent one of theirs as a standby. Or in case we decide to speed up operations."

"Just to keep level with Parky and Company? Or to get our section up first?"

There was a brief silence—just about long enough for the question to have traveled to the Moon and back.

"Really, Edith!" said Kato. "I was thinking of unexpected snags. Remember, we're not in a race—perish the thought! We've both promised ISA to lift between seven and fifteen April '12. We want to make sure we can meet the schedule—that's all."

"And will you?"

"Let me show you our little home movie—I'd appreciate it if you'd exit RECORD mode. This isn't the final version, so I'd like your comments at this stage."

The Japanese studios, Donald recalled, had a long and well-deserved reputation for model work and special effects. (How many times had Tokyo been destroyed by assorted monsters?) The detail of ship and seabed was so perfect that there was no sense of scale; anyone who did not know that visibility underwater was never more than a hundred meters—at best—might have thought that this was the real thing.

Titanic's crumpled rear section—about a third of her total length—lay on a flat, muddy plain surrounded by the debris that had rained down when the ship tore in two. The stern itself was in fairly good shape, though the deck had been partly peeled away, but farther forward it looked as if a giant hammer had smashed into the wreck. Only half of the rudder protruded from the seabed; two of the three enormous propellers were completely buried. Extricating *them* would be a major problem in itself.

"Looks a mess, doesn't it?" said Kato cheerfully. "But watch."

A shark swam leisurely past, suddenly noticed the imaginary camera, and departed in alarm. A nice touch, thought Donald, silently saluting the animators.

Now time speeded up. Numbers indicating days flickered on the right of the picture, twenty-four hours passing in every second. Slim girders descended from the liquid sky, and assembled themselves into an open framework surrounding the wreckage. Thick cables snaked into the shattered hulk.

Day Four Hundred—more than a year had passed. Now the water, hitherto quite invisible, was becoming milky. First the upper portion of the wreck, then the twisted plating of the hull, then everything down to the seabed itself, slowly disappeared into a huge block of glistening whiteness.

"Day Six Hundred," said Kato proudly. "Biggest ice cube in the world—except that it isn't quite cube-shaped. Think of all the refrigerators *that's* going to sell."

Maybe in Asia, thought Donald. But not in the U.K.—especially in Belfast. . . . Already there had been protests, cries of "sacrilege!" and even threats to boycott everything Japanese. Well, that was Kato's problem, and he was certainly well aware of it.

"Day Six Hundred Fifty. By this time, the seabed will also have consolidated, right down to several meters below the triple screws. Everything will be sealed tight in one solid block. All we have to do is lift it up to the surface. The ice will only provide a fraction of the buoyancy we need. So . . . ."

". . . so you'll ask Parky to sell you a few billion microspheres."

"Believe it or not, Donald, we *had* thought of making our own. But to copy Western technology? Perish the thought!"

"Then what *have* you invented instead?"

"Something very simple; we'll use a really hi-tech approach.

"Don't tell anyone yet—but we're going to bring the *Titanic* up with rockets."

25.
JASON
JUNIOR

THERE WERE TIMES when the International Seabed Authority's deputy director (Atlantic) had no official duties, because both halves of the *Titanic* operation were proceeding smoothly. But Jason Bradley was not the sort of man who enjoyed inaction.

Because he did not have to worry about tenure—the income on his investments was several times his ISA salary—he regarded himself as very much a free agent. Others might be trapped in their little boxes on the authority's organization chart; Jason Bradley roved at will, visiting any departments that looked interesting. Sometimes he informed the D.G., sometimes not. And usually he was welcomed, because his fame had spread before him, and other department heads regarded him more as an exotic visitor than a rival.

The other four deputy directors (Pacific, Indian, Antarctic, Arctic) all seemed willing enough to show him what was happening in their respective ocean empires. They were, of course, now united against a common enemy—the global rise in the sea level. After more than a decade of often acrimonious argument, it was now agreed that this rise was between one and two centimeters a year.

Bluepeace and other environmental groups put the blame on man; the scientists were not so sure. It was true that the billions of tons of CO_2 from thermal power plants and automobiles made *some* contribution to the notorious "Greenhouse Effect," but Mother Nature might still be the principal culprit; mankind's most heroic efforts could not match the pollution produced by one large volcano. All these arguments sounded very academic to peoples whose homes might cease to exist within their own lifetimes.

ISA chief scientist Franz Zwicker was widely regarded as the world's leading oceanographer—an opinion he made little effort to discourage. The first item most visitors noticed when entering his office was the *Time* magazine cover, with its caption "Admiral of the Ocean Sea." And no visitor escaped without a lecture, or at least a commercial, for Operation NEPTUNE.

"It's a scandal," Zwicker was fond of saying. "We have photo coverage of the Moon and Mars showing everything down to the size of a small house—but most of *our* planet is still completely unknown! They're spending billions to map the human genome, in the hope of triggering advances in medicine—someday. I don't doubt it; but mapping the seabed down to one-meter resolution would pay off immediately. Why, with camera and magnetometer we'd locate *all* the wrecks that have ever happened, since men started to build ships!"

To those who accused him of being a monomaniac, he was fond of giving Edward Teller's famous reply: "That's simply not true. I have *several* monomanias."

There was no doubt, however, that Operation NEPTUNE was the dominant one, and after some months' exposure to Zwicker, Bradley had begun to share it—at least when he was not preoccupied with *Titanic*.

The result, after months of brainstorming and gigabytes of CADCAMing, was Experimental Long-Range Autonomous Surveyor Mark I. The official acronym ELRAS survived only about a week; then, overnight, it was superseded. . . .

"He doesn't look much like his father," said Roy Emerson.

Bradley was getting rather tired of the joke, though for reasons which none of his colleagues—except the director-general—could have known. But he usually managed a sickly grin when displaying the lab's latest wonder to VVIPs. Mere VIPs were handled by the deputy director, Public Relations.

"No one will believe he's not named after me, but it's true. By pure coincidence, the U.S. Navy robot that made the first reconnaissance inside *Titanic* was called Jason Junior. So I'm afraid the name's stuck.

"But ISA's J.J. is very much more sophisticated—and completely independent. It can operate by itself, for days—or weeks—without any human intervention. Not like the first J.J., which was controlled through a cable; someone described it as a puppy on a leash. Well, we've slipped the leash; *this* J.J. can go hunting over all the world's ocean beds, sniffing at anything that looks interesting."

Jason Junior was not much larger than a man, and was shaped like a fat torpedo, with forward- and downward-viewing cameras. Main propulsion was provided by a single multibladed fan, and several small swivel jets gave attitude control. There were various streamlined bulges housing instruments, but none of the external manipulators found on most ROVs.

"What, no hands?" said Emerson.

"Doesn't need them—so we have a much cleaner design, with more speed and range. J.J.'s purely a surveyor; we can always go back later and look at anything interesting he finds on the seabed. Or under it, with his magnetometer and sonar."

Emerson was impressed; this was the sort of machine that appealed to his gadgeteering instincts. The short-lived fame that the Wave Wiper had brought him had long ago evaporated—though not, fortunately, the wealth that came with it.

He was, it seemed, a one-idea man; later inventions had all proved failures, and his well-publicized experiment to *drop* microspheres down to the *Titanic* in a hollow, air-filled tube had been an embarrassing debacle. Emerson's "hole in the sea" stubbornly refused to stay open; the descending spheres clogged it halfway, unless the flow was so small as to be useless.

The Parkinsons were quite upset, and had made poor Emerson feel uncomfortable at the last board meetings in ways that the English upper class had long perfected; for a few weeks, even his good friend Rupert had been distinctly cool.

But much worse was to come. A satirical Washington cartoonist had created a crazy "Thomas Alva Emerson" whose zany inventions would have put Rube Goldberg to shame. They had begun with the motorized zipper and proceeded via the digital toothbrush to the solar-powered pacemaker. By the time it had reached Braille speedometers for blind motorists, Roy Emerson had consulted his lawyer.

"Winning a libel action against a network," said Joe Wickram, "is about as easy as writing the Lord's Prayer on a rice grain with a felt pen. The defendant will plead fair comment, public interest, and quote at great length from the Bill of Rights. Of course," he added hopefully, "I'll be very happy to have a crack at it. I've always wanted to argue a case before the Supreme Court."

Very sensibly, Emerson had declined the offer, and at least something good had come out of the attack. The Parkinsons, to a man—and woman—felt it was unfair, and had rallied around him. Though they no longer took his engineering suggestions very seriously, they encouraged him to go on fact-finding missions like this one.

The authority's modest research and development center in Jamaica had no secrets, and was open to everybody. It was—in theory, at least—an impartial advisor to all who had dealings with the sea. The Parkinson and Nippon-Turner groups were now far and away the most publicly visible of these, and paid frequent visits to get advice on their own operations—and if possible, to check on the competition. They were careful to avoid scheduling conflicts, but sometimes there were slip-ups and polite "Fancy meeting *you* here!" exchanges. If Roy Emerson was not mistaken, he had noticed one of Kato's people in the departure lounge of Kingston Airport, just as he was arriving.

ISA, of course, was perfectly well aware of these undercurrents, and did its best to exploit them. Franz Zwicker was particularly adept at plugging his own projects—and getting other people to pay for them. Bradley was glad to cooperate, especially where J.J. was concerned, and was equally adept at giving little pep talks and handing out glossy brochures on Operation NEPTUNE.

". . . Once the software's been perfected," Bradley told Emerson, "so that he can avoid obstacles and deal with emergency situations, we'll let him loose. He'll be able to map the seabed in greater detail than anyone's ever done before. When the job's finished, he'll surface and we'll pick him up, recharge his batteries, and download his data. Then off he'll go again."

"Suppose he meets the great white shark?"

"We've even looked into that. Sharks seldom attack anything unfamiliar, and J.J. certainly doesn't look very appetizing. And his sonar and electromagnetic emissions will scare away most predators."

"Where do you plan to test him—and when?"

"Starting next month, on some well-mapped local sites.

Then out to the Continental Shelf. And then—up to the Grand Banks."

"I don't think you'll find much new around *Titanic*. Both sections have been photographed down to the square millimeter."

"That's true; we're not really interested in them. But J.J. can probe at least twenty meters below the seabed—and no one's ever done that for the debris field. God knows what's still buried there. Even if we don't find anything exciting, it will show J.J.'s capabilities—and give a big boost to the project. I'm going up to *Explorer* next week to make arrangements. It's ages since I was aboard her—and Parky—Rupert—says he has something to show me."

"He has indeed," said Emerson with a grin. "I shouldn't tell you this—but we've found the *real* treasure of the *Titanic*. Exactly where it was supposed to be."

26.
THE
MEDICI
GOBLET

"I WONDER IF you realize," Bradley shouted, to make himself heard above the roar and rattle of machinery, "what a bargain you've got. She cost almost a quarter billion to build—and that was back when a billion dollars was real money."

Rupert Parkinson was wearing an immaculate yachtsman's outfit which, especially when crowned by a hard hat, seemed a little out of place down here beside *Glomar Explorer*'s moon pool. The oily rectangle of water—larger than a tennis court—was surrounded by heavy salvage and handling equipment, much of it showing its age. Everywhere there were signs of hasty repairs, dabs of anticorrosion paint, and ominous notices saying OUT OF ORDER. Yet enough seemed to be working; Parkinson claimed they were actually ahead of schedule.

It's hard to believe, Bradley told himself, that it's almost thirty-five years since I stood here, looking down into this same black rectangle of water. I don't *feel* thirty-five years older . . . but I don't remember much about the callow youngster who'd just signed up for his first big job. Certainly he could never have dreamed of the one I'm holding down now.

It had turned out better than he had expected. After decades of battling with U.N. lawyers and a whole alphabet stew of government departments and environmental authorities, Bradley was learning that they were a necessary evil.

The Wild West days of the sea were over. There had been a brief time when there was very little law below a hundred fathoms; now he was sheriff, and, rather to his surprise, he was beginning to enjoy it.

One sign of his new status—some of his old colleagues called it "conversion"—was the framed certificate from Bluepeace he now had hanging on the office wall. It was right beside the photo presented to him years ago by the famous extinguisher of oil-rig fires, "Red" Adair. That bore the inscription: "Jason—isn't it great not to be bothered by life-insurance salesmen? Best wishes—Red."

The Bluepeace citation was somewhat more dignified:

TO JASON BRADLEY—IN RECOGNITION OF YOUR HUMANE TREATMENT OF A UNIQUE CREATURE, *OCTOPUS GIGANTEUS VERRILL*

At least once a month Bradley would leave his office and fly to Newfoundland—a province that was once more living up to its name. Since operations had started, more and more of world attention had been turned toward the drama being played out on the Grand Banks. The countdown to 2012 had begun, and bets were already being placed on the winner of "The Race for the *Titanic.*"

And there was another focus of interest, this time a morbid one. . . .

"What annoys me," said Parkinson, as they left the noisy and clamorous chaos of the moon pool, "are the ghouls who keep asking: 'Have you found any bodies yet?'"

"I'm always getting the same question. One day I'll answer: 'Yes—you're the first.'"

Parkinson laughed.

"Must try that myself. But here's the answer I give. You know that we're still finding boots and shoes lying on the seabed—in *pairs*, a few centimeters apart? Usually they're cheap and well worn, but last month we came across a beautiful example of the best English leatherwork. Looks as if they're straight from the cobbler—you can still read the label that says 'By Appointment to His Majesty.' Obviously one of the first-class passengers. . . .

"I've put them in a glass case in my office, and when I'm asked about bodies I point to them and say: 'Look—not even a scrap of bone left inside. It's a hungry world down there. The leather would have gone too, if it wasn't for the tannic acid.' That shuts them up very quickly."

Glomar Explorer had not been designed for gracious living, but Rupert Parkinson had managed to transform one of the aft staterooms, just below the helipad, into a fair imitation of a luxury hotel suite. It reminded Bradley of their first meeting, back in Picadilly—ages ago, it now seemed. The room contained one item, however, which was more than a little out of place in such surroundings.

It was a wooden chest, about a meter high, and it appeared almost new. But as he approached, Bradley recognized a familiar and unmistakable odor—the metallic tang of iodine, proof of long immersion in the sea. Some diver—was it Cousteau?—had once used the phrase "The scent of treasure." Here it was, hanging in the air—and setting the blood pounding in his veins.

"Congratulations, Rupert. So you've got into Great-Grandfather's suite."

"Yes. Two of the Deep ROVs entered a week ago and did a preliminary survey. This is the first item they brought out."

The chest still displayed, in stenciled lettering unfaded after a century in the abyss, a somewhat baffling inscription:

BROKEN ORANGE PEKOE

UPPER GLENCAIRN ESTATE

MATAKELLE

Parkinson raised the lid, almost reverently, and then drew aside the sheet of metal foil beneath it.

"Standard eighty-pound Ceylon tea chest," he said. "It happened to be the right size, so they simply repacked it. And I'd no idea they used aluminium foil, back in 1912! Of course, the B.O.P. wouldn't fetch a very good price at Colombo auction now—but it did its job. Admirably."

With a piece of stiff cardboard, Parkinson delicately cleared away the top layer of the soggy black mess; he looked, Bradley thought, exactly like an underwater archaeologist extracting a fragment of pottery from the seabed. This, however, was no twenty-five-century-old Greek amphora, but something far more sophisticated.

"The Medici Goblet," Parkinson whispered almost reverently. "No one has seen it for a hundred years; no one *ever* expected to see it again."

He exposed only the upper few inches, but that was enough to show a circle of glass inside which multicolored threads were embedded in a complex design.

"We won't remove it until we're on land," said Parkinson, "but this is what it looks like."

He opened a typical coffee-table art book, bearing the title

Glories of Venetian Glass. The full-page photo showed what at first sight looked like a glittering fountain, frozen in midair.

"I don't believe it," said Bradley, after a few seconds of wide-eyed astonishment. "How could anyone actually drink from it? More to the point, how could anyone *make* it?"

"Good questions. First of all, it's purely ornamental—intended to be looked at, not used. A perfect example of Wilde's dictum: 'All art is quite useless.'

"And I wish I could answer your second question. *We just don't know.* Oh, of course we can guess at some of the techniques used—but how did the glassblower make those curlicues intertwine? And look at the way those little spheres are nested one inside the other! If I hadn't seen them with my own eyes, I'd have sworn that some of these pieces could only have been assembled in zero gravity."

"So *that's* why Parkinson's booked space on Skyhab 3."

"What a ridiculous rumor; not worth contradicting."

"Roy Emerson told me he was looking forward to his first trip into space . . . and setting up a weightless lab."

"I'll fax Roy a polite note, telling him to keep his bloody mouth shut. But since you've raised the subject—yes, we think there are possibilities for zero-gee glassblowing. It may not start a revolution in the industry, like float glass back in the last century—but it's worth a try."

"This probably isn't a polite question, but how much is this goblet worth?"

"I assume you're not asking in your official capacity, so I won't give a figure I'd care to put in a company report. Anyway, you know how crazy the art business is—more ups and downs than the stock market! Look at those late Twentieth-Century megadollar daubs you can't give away now. And in this case there's the history of the piece—how can you put a value on *that*?"

"Make a guess."

"I'd be very disappointed at anything less than fifty M."

Bradley whistled.

"And how much more is down there?"

"Lots. Here's the complete listing, prepared for the exhibition the Smithsonian had planned. *Is* planning—just a hundred years late."

There were more than forty items on the list, all with highly technical Italianate descriptions. About half had question marks beside them.

"Bit of a mystery here," said Parkinson. "Twenty-two of the pieces are missing—but we *know* they were aboard, and we're sure G.G. had them in his suite, because he complained about the space they were taking up—he couldn't throw a party."

"So—going to blame the French again?"

It was an old joke, and rather a bitter one. Some of the French expeditions to the wreck, in the years following its 1985 discovery, had done considerable damage while attempting to recover artifacts. Ballard and his associates had never forgiven them.

"No. I guess they've a pretty good alibi; we're definitely the first inside. My theory is that G.G. had them moved out into an adjoining suite or corridor—I'm sure they're not far away—we'll find them sooner or later."

"I hope so; if your estimate is right—and after all, you're the expert—those boxes of glass will pay for this whole operation. And everything else will be a pure bonus. Nice work, Rupert."

"Thank you. We hope Phase Two goes equally well."

"The Mole? I noticed it down beside the moon pool. Anything since your last report—which was rather sketchy?"

"I know. We were in the middle of urgent mods when your

office started making rude noises about schedules and deadlines. But now we're on top of the problem—I hope."

"Do you still plan to make a test first, on a stretch of open seabed?"

"No. We're going to go for broke; we're confident that all systems are okay, so why wait? Do you remember what happened in the Apollo Program, back in '68? One of the most daring technological gambles in history. . . . The big Saturn V had only flown twice—unmanned—and the second flight had been a partial failure. Yet NASA took a calculated risk; the next flight was not only manned—it went straight to the Moon!

"Of course, we're not playing for such high stakes, but if the Mole doesn't work—or we lose it—we're in real trouble; our whole operation depends on it. The sooner we know about any real problems, the better.

"No one's ever tried something quite like this before; but our first run will be the real thing—and we'd like you to watch.

"Now, Jason—how about a nice cup of tea?"

27.

INJUNCTION

Article 1
Use of terms and scope

1. For the purposes of this Convention:

(1) "Area" means the seabed and ocean floor and subsoil thereof, beyond the limits of national jurisdiction;

(2) "Authority" means the International Seabed Authority;

Article 145
Protection of the marine environment

Necessary measures shall be taken in accordance with this Convention with respect to activities in the Area to ensure effective protection for the marine environment from harmful effects which may arise from such activities. To this end the Authority shall adopt appropriate rules, regulations and procedures for *inter alia*:

    (a) the prevention, reduction and control of pollution and other hazards to the marine environment . . . particular attention being paid to the need for protection from harmful effects of such activities as drilling, dredging, disposal of waste, construction and operation or maintenance of installations, pipelines, and other devices related to such activities.

(United Nations Convention on the Law of the Sea, 1982)

"WE'RE IN DEEP TROUBLE," said Kato, from his Tokyo office, "and that's not meant to be funny."

"What's the problem?" asked Donald Craig, relaxing in the Castle garden. From time to time he liked to give his eyes a chance of focusing on something more than half a meter away, and this was an unusually warm and sunny afternoon for early spring.

"Bluepeace. They've lodged another protest with ISA—and this time I'm afraid they've got a case."

"I thought we'd settled all this."

"So did we; heads are rolling in our legal department. We can do everything we'd planned—except actually *raise* the wreck."

"It's a little late in the day to discover that, isn't it? And you've never told me how you intended to get the extra lift. Of course, I never took that crack about rockets seriously."

"Sorry about that—we'd been negotiating with Dupont and Thiokol and Union Carbide and half a dozen others—didn't want to talk until we were certain of our supplier."

"Of what?"

"Hydrazine. Rocket monopropellant. So I wasn't economizing too greatly with the truth."

"Hydrazine? Now where— Of course! That's how Cussler brought her up, in *Raise the Titanic!*"

"Yes, and it's quite a good idea—it decomposes into pure

nitrogen and hydrogen, plus lots of heat. But Cussler didn't have to cope with Bluepeace. They got wind of what we were doing—wish I knew how—and claim that hydrazine is a dangerous poison, and some is bound to be spilled, however carefully we handle it, and so on and so forth."

"*Is* it a poison?"

"Well, I'd hate to drink it. Smells like concentrated ammonia, and probably tastes worse."

"So what are you going to do?"

"Fight, of course. And think of alternatives. Parky will be laughing his head off."

28.
MOLE

THE THREE-MAN DEEP-SEA SUBMERSIBLE *Marvin* had been intended as the successor of the famous *Alvin*, which had played such a key role in the first exploration of the wreck. *Alvin*, however, showed no intention of retiring, though almost every one of its original components had long since been replaced.

Marvin was also much more comfortable than its progenitor, and had greater reserves of power. No longer was it necessary to spend a boring two and a half hours in free-fall to the seabed; with the help of its motors, *Marvin* could reach the *Titanic* in less than an hour. And in an emergency, by jettisoning all external equipment, the titanium sphere holding the crew could get back to the surface in minutes—an incompressible air bubble ascending from the depths.

For Bradley, this was a double first. He had never yet seen the *Titanic* with his own eyes, and though he had handled *Marvin* on test and training runs down to a few hundred meters, he had never taken it right down to the bottom. Needless to say, he was carefully watched by the submersible's usual pilot, who was doing his best not to be a backseat driver.

"Altitude two hundred meters. Wreck bearing one two zero."

Altitude! That was a word that sounded strangely in a diver's ear. But here inside *Marvin*'s life-support sphere, depth was almost irrelevant. What really concerned Bradley was his elevation above the seabed, and keeping enough clearance to avoid obstacles. He felt that he was piloting not a submarine but a low-flying aircraft—one searching for landmarks in a thick fog. . . .

"Searching," however, was hardly the right word, for he knew exactly where his target was. The brilliant echo on the sonar display was dead ahead, and now only a hundred meters away. In a moment the TV camera would pick it up, but Bradley wanted to use his own eyes. He was not a child of the video age, to whom nothing was quite real until it had appeared on a screen.

And there was the knife edge of the prow, looming up in the glare of *Marvin*'s lights. Bradley cut the motor, and let his little craft drift slowly toward the converging cliffs of steel.

Now he was separated from the *Titanic* by only a few centimeters of adamantine crystal, bearing a pressure that it was not wise to dwell upon. He was confronting the ghost that had haunted the Atlantic sea lanes for almost a century; it still seemed to be driving ahead under its own power, as if on a voyage that, even now, had only just begun.

The enormous anchor, half hidden by its drapery of weeds, was still patiently waiting to be lowered. It almost dwarfed *Marvin*, and its dangling tons of mass appeared so ominous that Bradley gave it a wide berth as he cruised slowly down the line of portholes, staring blankly into nothingness like the empty eye sockets of a skull.

He had almost forgotten the purpose of his mission, when the voice from the world above jolted him back to reality.

"*Explorer* to *Marvin*. We're waiting."

"Sorry—just admiring the view. She *is* impressive—cameras don't do her justice. You've got to see her for yourself."

This was an old argument, which as far as Bradley was concerned had been settled long ago. Though robots and their electronic sensors were invaluable—indeed, absolutely essential—both for reconnaissance and actual operations, they could never give the whole picture. "Telepresence" was marvelous, but it could sometimes be a dangerous illusion. You might believe you were experiencing a hundred percent of some remote reality but it was only ninety-five percent—and that remaining five percent could be vital: men had died because there was still no good way of transmitting those warning signals that only the sense of smell could detect. Although he had seen thousands of stills and videos of the wreck, only now did Bradley feel that he was beginning to understand it.

He was reluctant to tear himself away, and realized how frustrated Robert Ballard must have been when he had only seconds for *his* first sighting of the wreck. Then he actuated the bow thrusters, swung *Marvin* away from the towering metal cliff, and headed toward his real target.

The Mole was resting on a cradle about twenty meters from *Titanic,* pointing downward at a forty-five-degree angle. It looked rather like a spaceship headed in the wrong direction, and there had been many deplorable ethnic jokes about launchpads built by the engineers of certain small European countries.

The conical drilling head was already deeply buried in the sediment, and a few meters of the broad metal tape that was the Mole's "payload" lay stretched out on the seabed behind it. Bradley moved *Marvin* into position to get a good view, and switched the video recorders to high speed.

"We're ready," he reported to topside. "Start the count-down."

"We're holding at T minus ten seconds. Inertial guidance

running . . . seven . . . six . . . five . . . four . . .
three . . . two . . . one . . . liftoff! Sorry—I mean, dig
in!"

The drill had started to spin, and almost at once the Mole
was hidden by clouds of silt. However, Bradley could see that it
was disappearing with surprising speed; in only a matter of
seconds it had vanished into the seabed.

"You've cleared the tower," he reported, keeping the spirit
of the occasion. "Can't see anything—the launchpad's hidden by
smoke. Well, mud. . . ."

"Now it's settling. The Mole's vanished. Just a little crater,
slowly filling in. We'll head around the other side to meet it."

"Take your time. Quickest estimate is thirty minutes.
Longest is fifty. Quite a few bets riding on this baby."

And quite a few million dollars as well, thought Bradley, as
he piloted *Marvin* toward *Titanic*'s prow. If the Mole gets stuck
before it can complete its mission, Parky and company will have
to go back to the drawing board.

He was waiting on the port side when the Mole resurfaced
after forty-five minutes. It was not attempting any speed
records; its maiden voyage had been a complete success.

Now the first of the planned thirty belts, each capable of
lifting a thousand tons, had been safely emplaced. When the
operation had been completed, *Titanic* could be lifted off the
ocean floor, like a melon in a string bag.

That was the theory, and it seemed to be working. Florida
was still a long way off, but now it had come just a little closer.

29.
SARCOPHAGUS

"WE'VE FOUND IT!"

Roy Emerson had never seen Rupert Parkinson in so exuberant a mood; it was positively un-English.

"Where?" he asked. "Are you sure?"

"Ninety-nine—well, ninety-five percent. Just where I expected. There was an unoccupied suite—wasn't ready in time for the voyage. On the same deck as G.G. and only a few yards away. Both doors are jammed so we'll have to cut our way in. The ROV's going down now to have a crack at it. You should have been here."

Perhaps, thought Emerson. But this is a family affair, and he would feel an interloper. Besides, it might be a false alarm—like most rumors of sunken treasure.

"How long before you get inside?"

"Shouldn't take more than an hour—it's fairly thin steel, and we'll be through it in no time."

"Well, good luck. Keep me in the picture."

Roy Emerson went back to what he pretended was work. He felt guilty when he was not inventing something, which was now most of the time. Trying to reduce the electronic chaos of his data banks by rearranging and reclassifying did give the illusion of useful employment.

And so he missed all the excitement.

The little group in Rupert's suite aboard *Glomar Explorer* was so intent upon the monitor screen that their drinks were virtually ignored—no great hardship, because according to long tradition on such vessels, they were nonalcoholic.

A record number of Parkinsons—almost a quorum, someone had pointed out—had assembled for this occasion. Though few shared Rupert's confidence, it had been a good excuse to visit the scene of operations. Only George had been here before; William, Arnold, and Gloria were all newcomers. The rest of the group watching ROV 3 gliding silently across *Titanic*'s deck were ship's officers and senior engineers, recruited from half a dozen ocean-oriented firms.

"Have you noticed," somebody whispered, "how the weeds have grown? Must be due to our lights—she wasn't like this when we started ops—bridge looks like the Hanging Gardens of Babylon. . . ."

There was very little other comment, still less any conversation, as ROV 3 dropped down into the yawning cavity of the grand staircase. A century ago, elegant ladies and their sleek escorts had strolled up and down the thick-piled carpet, never dreaming of their fate—or imagining that in little more than two years the guns of August would put an end to the gilded Edwardian Age they so perfectly epitomized.

ROV 3 turned into the main starboard corridor on the promenade deck, past the rows of first-class staterooms. It was moving very slowly in these confined quarters, and the TV image was now limited to freeze-frame black and white, with a new picture every two seconds.

All data and control signals were now being relayed over an

ultrasonic link through a repeater placed on the deck. From time to time there were annoying holdups, when the screen went blank and the only indication of ROV 3's continued existence was a high-pitched whistle. Some obstacle was absorbing the carrier wave, causing a momentary break in the connection. There would be a brief interval of electronic "handshaking" and error correction; then the picture would return and ROV 3's pilot, four kilometers above, could resume progress. These interruptions did nothing to lessen the suspense; it had been several minutes before anyone in Parkinson's suite had said a word.

There was a universal sigh of relief as the robot came to rest outside a plain, unmarked door, its white paint blindingly brilliant in ROV 3's floodlights. The decorators might have left only yesterday; apart from a few flakes that had peeled away, almost all the paint was still intact.

Now ROV 3 began the tricky but essential task of anchoring itself to the job—a procedure just as important underwater as in space. First it blasted two explosive bolts through the door, and clamped itself on to them, so it was rigidly attached to the working area.

The glare of the oxy-arc thermal lance flooded the corridor, making ROV 3's own lights seem feeble in comparison. The thin metal of the door offered no resistance as the incandescent knife—favorite tool of generations of safecrackers—sliced through it. In less than five minutes, a circle almost a meter wide had been carved out, and fell slowly forward, knocking up a small cloud of silt as it hit the floor.

ROV 3 unclamped itself, and rose a few centimeters so it could peer into the hole. The image flickered, then stabilized as the automatic exposure adjusted to the new situation.

Almost at once, Rupert Parkinson gave a hoot of delight.

"There they are!" he cried. "Just as I said—one . . .

two . . . three-four-five . . . swing the camera over to the right—six . . . seven—a little higher . . . *My God—what's that?"*

No one ever remembered who screamed first.

30.
PIETÀ

JASON BRADLEY HAD SEEN something like this before, in a space movie whose name he couldn't recall. There had been a dead astronaut cradled in mechanical arms, being carried toward the stars. . . . But this robot pietà was rising from the Atlantic depths, toward the circling inflatable boats waiting to receive it.

"That's the last one," said Parkinson somberly. "The girl. We still don't know her name."

Just like those Russian sailors, thought Bradley, who had been laid out on this very same deck, more than thirty years ago. He could not avoid it; the silly cliché flashed into his mind: "This is where I came in."

And, like many of the sailors brought up in Operation JENNIFER, these dead also appeared to be only sleeping. That was the most amazing—indeed, uncanny—aspect of the whole matter, which had seized the imagination of the world. After all the trouble we went to, explaining why there couldn't possibly be even a scrap of bone. . . .

"I'm surprised," he said to Parkinson, "that you were able to identify any of them, after all these years."

"Contemporary newspapers—family albums—even poor

Irish immigrants usually had at least one photo taken during their lifetime. Especially when they were leaving home forever. I don't think there's an attic in Ireland the media haven't ransacked in the last couple of days."

ROV 3 had handed over its burden to the rubber-suited divers circling in their inflatables. They lifted it carefully—tenderly—into the cradle suspended over the side from one of *Explorer*'s cranes. It was obviously very light; one man was able to handle it easily.

With a common, unspoken impulse both Parkinson and Bradley moved away from the rail; they had seen enough of this sad ritual. During the past forty-eight hours, five men and one woman had been brought out of the tomb in which they had been lying for almost a century—apparently beyond the reach of time.

When they were together in Parkinson's suite, Bradley handed over a small computer module. "It's all there," he said. "The ISA lab's been working overtime. There are still some puzzling details, but the general picture seems clear.

"I don't know if you ever heard the story about *Alvin*—in the early days of its career, it was lost in deep water. The crew just managed to scramble out—leaving their lunch behind.

"When the sub was salvaged a couple of years later, the crew's lunch was *exactly* as they'd left it. That was the first hint that in cold water, with low oxygen content, organic decay can be vanishingly slow.

"And they've recovered bodies from wrecks in the Great Lakes that look absolutely fresh after decades—you can still see the expressions of surprise on the sailors' faces!

"So," continued Bradley, "the first requirement is that the corpse be in a sealed environment, where marine organisms can't get at it. That's what happened here; these people were trapped when they tried to find a way out—poor devils, they must have been lost in first-class territory! They'd broken the lock on the other door of the suite—but couldn't open the other before the water reached them. . . .

"But there's more to it than cold, stagnant water—and this is the really fascinating part of the story. Have you ever heard of bog people?"

"No," said Parkinson.

"Neither had I, until yesterday. But from time to time Danish archaeologists keep finding almost perfectly preserved corpses—victims of sacrifices, apparently—more than a *thousand* years old. Every wrinkle, every hair intact—they look like incredibly detailed sculptures. The reason? They were buried in peat bogs, and the tannin protected them from decay. Remember the boots and shoes found scattered around the wreck—all the leather untouched?"

Parkinson was no fool, though he sometimes pretended to be a character out of P. G. Wodehouse; it took him only seconds to make the connection.

"Tannin? But how? Of course—the tea chests!"

"Exactly; several of them had been breached by the impact. But our chemists say tannin may be only part of the story. The ship had been newly painted, of course—so the water samples we've analyzed show considerable amounts of arsenic and lead. A mighty unhealthy environment for any bacteria."

"I'm sure that's the answer," said Parkinson. "What an extraordinary twist of fate! That tea did a lot better than anyone ever imagined—or *could* imagine. . . . And I'm afraid G.G. has brought us some very bad luck. Just when things were going smoothly."

Bradley knew exactly what he meant. To the old charge of desecrating a historic shrine had now been added that of grave robbing. And, by a strange paradox, an apparently fresh grave at that.

The long-forgotten Thomas Conlin, Patrick Dooley, Martin Gallagher, and their three as-yet-still-anonymous companions had transformed the whole situation.

It was a paradox which, surely, would delight any true Irishman. With the discovery of her dead, *Titanic* had suddenly come alive.

31.
A MATTER
OF
MEGAWATTS

"WE HAVE THE ANSWER," said a tired but triumphant Kato.

"I wonder if it matters now," answered Donald Craig.

"Oh, all that hysteria isn't going to last. Our P.R. boys are already hard at work—and so are Parky's. We've had a couple of summit meetings to plan a joint strategy. We may even turn it to our mutual advantage."

"I don't see—"

"Obvious! Thanks to *our*— Well, Parky's—careful exploring, these poor folk will at last get a Christian burial, back in their own country. The Irish will love it. Don't tell anyone, but we're already talking to the Pope."

Donald found Kato's flippant approach more than a little offensive. It would certainly upset Edith, who seemed fascinated by the lovely child-woman the world had named Colleen.

"You'd better be careful. Some of them may be Protestant."

"Not likely. They all boarded in the deep south, didn't they?"

"Yes—at Queenstown. You won't find it on the map, though—a name like that wasn't popular after Independence. Now it's called Cobh."

"How do you spell that?"

"C-O-B-H."

"Well, we'll talk to the archbishops, or whoever, as well as the cardinals, just to cover all bases. But let me tell you what our engineers have cooked up. If it works, it will be a lot better than hydrazine. And it should even start Bluepeace shouting slogans for *us*."

"That'll be a nice change. In fact, a miracle."

"Miracles are our business—didn't you know?"

"What are the specs of this particular one?"

"First, we're making our iceberg larger, to get more lift. As a result, we'll only need about ten k-tons of extra buoyancy. We *could* go Parky's route for that, and at first we were afraid we might have to. But there's a neater—and cleaner—way of getting gas down there. *Electrolysis.* Splitting the water into oxygen and hydrogen."

"That's an old idea. Won't it take enormous amounts of current? And what about the risk of an explosion?"

"Silly question, Donald. The gases will go to separate electrodes, and we'll have a membrane to keep them apart. But you're right about the current. Gigawatt-hours! But we've got them—when our nuclear subs have done their thing with the Peltier cooling elements, we'll switch to electrolysis. May have to rent another boat, though—why are subs always called boats? I told you that the Brits and the French would like to get into the act, so *that's* no problem."

"Very elegant," said Donald. "And I see what you mean about pleasing Bluepeace. Everyone's in favor of oxygen."

"Exactly—and when we vent the balloons on the way up, the whole world will breathe a little easier. At least, that's what P.R. will be saying."

"And the hydrogen will go straight up to the stratosphere without bothering anyone. Oh—what about the poor old ozone layer? Any danger of making more holes?"

"We've checked that, of course. Won't be any worse off than it is now. Which, I admit, isn't saying a great deal."

"Would it make sense to *bottle* the gases on the way up? You're starting with hundreds of tons of oxy-hydrogen, at four hundred atmospheres. That must be quite valuable; why throw it away?"

"Yes—we've even looked into that. It's marginal—increased complexity, cost of shipping tanks, and so on. Might be worth a try on a test basis—and gives us a fall-back position if the environment lobby gets nasty again."

"You've thought of everything, haven't you?" said Donald with frank admiration.

Kato shook his head slowly.

"Our friend Bradley once told me: 'When you've thought of everything—the sea will think of something else.' Words of wisdom, and I've never forgotten them. . . . Must hang up now— Oh—give my love to Edith."

OPERATIONS

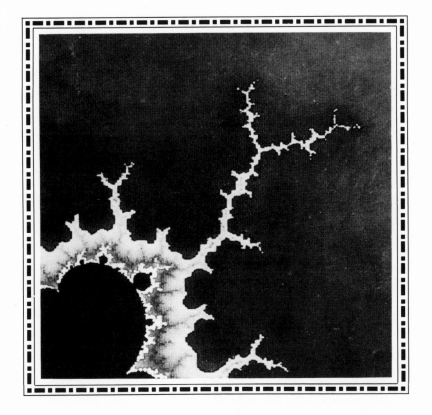

32.
NOBODY
HERE BUT
US ROBOTS

UNTIL THE FIRST DECADE of the new century, the great wreck and the debris surrounding it had remained virtually unchanged, though not untouched. Now, as 2010 approached, it was a hive of activity—or, rather, two hives, a thousand meters apart.

The framework of scaffolding around the bow section was almost complete, and the Mole had successfully laid twenty-five of the massive straps under the hull; there were only five to go. Most of the mud that had piled up around the prow when it drove into the seabed had been blasted away by powerful water jets, and the huge anchors were no longer half buried in silt.

More than twenty thousand tons of buoyancy had already been provided by as many cubic meters of packaged microspheres, strategically placed around the framework, and at the few places inside the wreck where the structure could safely take the strain. But *Titanic* had not stirred from her resting place—nor was she supposed to. Another ten thousand tons of lift would be needed to get her out of the mud, and to start her on the long climb to the surface.

As for the shattered stern—that had already disappeared inside a slowly accreting block of ice. The media were fond of quoting Hardy's "In shadowy silent distance grew the Iceberg too"—even though the poet could never have imagined this application of his words.

The penultimate verse was also quoted widely, and equally out of context. Both the Parkinson and Nippon-Turner consortia were rather tired of being told that

> They were bent
> By paths coincident
> On being anon twin halves of one august event

They hoped that it would be "august"—but not, if they could possibly help it, coincident.

Virtually all the work on both portions of the wreck had been carried out by remote control from the surface; only in critical cases were human beings actually required on the site. During the past decade, underwater robot technology had been pushed far beyond even the remarkable achievements of the previous century's offshore oil operations. The payoff would be enormous—although, as Rupert Parkinson often wryly remarked, most of it would go to other people.

There had, of course, been problems, mishaps—even accidents, though none involving loss of life. During one severe winter storm, *Explorer* had been forced to abandon station, much to the disgust of her captain, who considered this a professional insult. His vomitous passengers did not altogether appreciate his point of view.

Even this display of North Atlantic ferocity, however, had not interrupted operations on the stern. Two hundred meters down, the demobilized nuclear submarines, now rechristened, after a pioneer oceanographer and a famous shipbuilder, *Matthew Fontaine Maury* and *Peter the Great*, were scarcely aware of the storm. Their reactors continued steadily pouring megawatt upon megawatt of low-voltage current down to the seabed—creating a rising column of warm water in the process, as heat was pumped out of the wreck.

This artificial upwelling had produced an unexpected bonus, by bringing to the surface nutrients that would otherwise have been trapped on the seabed. The resulting plankton bloom was much appreciated by the local fish population, and the last cod harvest had been a record one. The government of Newfoundland had formally requested the submarines to remain on station, even when they had fulfilled their contract with Nippon-Turner.

Quite apart from all this activity off the Grand Banks, a great deal of money and effort was being expended thousands of kilometers away. Down in Florida, not far from the launchpads that had seen men leave for the Moon—and were now seeing them prepare to go to Mars—dredging and construction for the *Titanic* Underwater Museum was well under way. And on the other side of the globe, Tokyo-on-Sea was preparing an even more elaborate display, with transparent viewing corridors for visitors and, of course, continuous performances of what was hoped would be a truly spectacular movie.

Vast sums of money were also being gambled elsewhere—especially in the land once more called Russia. Thanks to *Peter the Great*, share dealings in *Titanic* spinoff companies were very popular on the Moscow Stock Exchange.

33.
SOLAR
MAX

"ANOTHER OF MY MONOMANIAS," said Franz Zwicker, "is the sunspot cycle. Especially the current one."

"What's particular about it?" asked Bradley, as they walked down to the lab together.

"First of all, it will peak in—you guessed it!—2012. It's already way past the 1990 maximum, and getting close to the 2001 record."

"So?"

"Well, between you and me, I'm scared. So many cranks have tried to correlate events with the eleven-year cycle—which isn't always eleven years anyway!—that sunspot counting sometimes gets classed with astrology. But there's no doubt that the sun influences practically everything on Earth. I'm sure it's responsible for the weird weather we've been having during the last quarter century. To some extent, anyway; we can't put *all* the blame on the human race, much as Bluepeace and Company would like to."

"I thought you were supposed to be on their side!"

"Only on Mondays, Wednesdays, and Fridays. The rest of the week I keep a wary eye on Mother Nature. And the weather patterns aren't the only abnormality. Seismic activity seems to be increasing. Look at California. Why do people *still* build houses in San Francisco? Wasn't 2002 bad enough? And we're *still* waiting for the Big One. . . ."

Jason felt privileged to share the scientist's thoughts; the two men, so different in background and character, had grown to respect each other.

"And there's something else, that occasionally gives me nightmares. Deep-water blowouts—perhaps triggered by earthquakes. Or even by man."

"I've known several. A big one in '98, in the Louisiana Field. Wrote off a whole rig."

"Oh, that was just a mild burp! I'm talking about the real thing—like that crater the Shell Oil scientists found two kilometers down in the Gulf, back in the eighties. Imagine the explosion that caused *that*—three million tons of seabed scooped out! Equivalent to a good-sized atomic bomb."

"And you think that could happen again?"

"I *know* it will—but not when and where. I keep warning the people up at Hibernia that they're tickling the dragon's tail. If Tommy Gold is right—and he was right about neutron stars, even if he struck out on moondust and the Steady State!—we've barely scratched the Earth's crust. Everything we've tapped so far is just minor leakage from the *real* hydrocarbon reservoirs, ten or more kilometers down."

"Some leak! It's been running our civilization for the last couple of centuries."

"Did you say running—or ruining? Well, here's your prize pupil. How's class going?"

J.J. lay in a transporter cradle, very much a fish out of water. It was attached to a bank of computers by what seemed to Bradley to be an absurdly thin cable. Having grown up with copper wiring, he had never become quite accustomed to the fiber-optic revolution.

Nothing seemed to be happening; the technician in charge hastily concealed the microbook she was viewing, and quickly scanned the monitor display.

"Everything fine, Doctor," she said cheerfully. "Just verifying the expert system data bases."

That's part of *me*, thought Jason. He had spent hours in dive simulators, while computer programmers tried to codify and record his hard-won skills—the very essence of veteran ocean engineer J. Bradley. He was beginning to feel more and more that, at least in a psychological sense, J.J. was becoming a surrogate son.

That feeling became strongest when they were engaged in a direct conversation. It was an old joke in the trade that divers had a vocabulary of only a couple of hundred words—which was all they needed for their work. J.J. had enough artificial intelligence to exceed this by a comfortable margin.

The lab had hoped to surprise Jason by using his voice as a template for J.J.'s speech synthesizer, but his reaction had been disappointing. The pranksters had forgotten that few people can recognize their own recorded voice, especially if it is uttering sentences that they have never spoken themselves. Jason had not caught on until he had noticed the grinning faces around him.

"Any reason, Anne, why we can't start the wet run on schedule?" Zwicker asked.

"No, Doctor. The emergency recall algorithm still doesn't seem to be working properly, but of course we won't need it for the tests."

Although the sound transducers were not designed to function in air, Jason could not resist a few words with Junior.

"Hello, J.J. Can you hear me?"

"I can hear you."

The words were badly distorted, but quite recognizable. Underwater, the speech quality would be much better.

"Do you recognize me?"

There was a long silence. Then J.J. replied.

"Question not understood."

"Walk closer, Mr. Bradley," the technician advised. "He's very deaf out of water."

"Do you recognize me?"

"Yes. You are John Maxwell."

"Back to the drawing board," muttered Zwicker.

"And who," asked Bradley, more amused than annoyed, "is John Maxwell?"

The girl was quite embarrassed.

"He's section chief, Voice Recognition. But there's no problem—this isn't a fair test. Underwater he'll know you from half a kilometer away."

"I hope so. Goodbye, J.J. See you later—when you're not quite so deaf. Let's see if Deep Jeep is in better shape."

Deep Jeep was the lab's other main project, in some ways almost equally demanding. The reaction of most visitors at first viewing was: "Is it a submarine or a diving suit?" And the answer was always, "Both."

Servicing and operating three-man deep submersibles like *Marvin* was an expensive business: a single dive could cost a hundred thousand dollars. But there were many occasions when a much less elaborate, one-man vehicle would be adequate.

Jason Bradley's secret ambition was already well known to the entire lab. He hoped Deep Jeep would be ready in time to take him down to *Titanic*—while the wreck still lay on the ocean floor.

34.
STORM

IT WOULD BE DECADES BEFORE the meteorologists could prove that the great storm of 2010 was one of the series that had begun in the 1980s, heralding the climatic changes of the next millennium. Before it exhausted its energies battering against the western ramparts of the Alps, Gloria did twenty billion dollars' worth of damage and took more than a thousand lives.

The weather satellites, of course, gave a few hours' warning—otherwise the death toll would have been even greater. But, inevitably, there were many who did not hear the forecasts, or failed to take them seriously. Especially in Ireland, which was the first to receive the hammerblow from the heavens.

Donald and Edith Craig were editing the latest footage from Operation DEEP FREEZE when Gloria hit Conroy Castle. They heard and felt nothing deep inside the massive walls—not even the crash when the camera obscura was swept off the battlements.

Ada now cheerfully admitted that she was hopeless at *pure* mathematics—the kind which, in G. H. Hardy's famous toast, would never be of any use to anyone. Unknown to him—because the secrets of ENIGMA's code-breaking were not revealed until decades later—Hardy had been proved spectacularly wrong during his own lifetime. In the hands of Alan Turing and his colleagues, even something as abstract as number theory could win a war.

Most of calculus and higher trigonometry, and virtually all of symbolic logic, were closed books to Ada. She simply wasn't interested; her heart was in geometry and the properties of space. Already she was trifling with five dimensions, four having proved too simple. Like Newton, much of the time she was "sailing strange seas of thought—alone."

But today, she was back in ordinary three-space, thanks to the present that "Uncle" Bradley had just sent her. Thirty years after its first appearance, Rubik's Cube had made a comeback—in a far more deadly mutation.

Because it was a purely mechanical device, the original cube had one weakness, for which its addicts were sincerely thankful. Unlike all their neighbors, the six *center* squares on each face were fixed. The other forty-eight squares could orbit around them, to create a possible 43252 00327 44898 56000 distinct patterns.

The Mark II had no such limitations; all the fifty-four squares were capable of movement, so there were no fixed centers to give reference points to its maddened manipulators. Only the development of microchips and liquid crystal displays had made such a prodigy possible; nothing *really* moved, but the multicolored squares could be dragged around the face of the cube merely by touching them with a fingertip.

Relaxing in her little boat with Lady, engrossed with her new toy, Ada had been slow to notice the darkening sky. The storm was almost upon her before she started the electric motor and headed for shelter. That there could be any danger never occurred to her; after all, Lake Mandelbrot was only three feet deep. But she disliked getting wet—and Lady *hated* it.

By the time she had reached the lake's first western lobe, the roar of the gale was almost deafening. Ada was thrilled; this was really exciting! But Lady was terrified, and tried to hide herself under the seat.

Heading down the Spike, between the avenue of cypresses, she was partly sheltered from the full fury of the gale. But for the first time, she became alarmed; the great trees on either side were swaying back and forth like reeds.

She was only a dozen meters from the safety of the boathouse, far into the Utter West of the M-Set and nearing the infinity border post at minus 1.999, when Patrick O'Brian's fears about the transplanted cypress trees were tragically fulfilled.

35.
ARTIFACT

One of the most moving archaeological discoveries ever made took place in Israel in 1976, during a series of excavations carried out by scientists from the Hebrew University and the French Center for Prehistoric Research in Jerusalem.

At a 10,000-year-old campsite, they uncovered the skeleton of a child, one hand pressed against its cheek. In that hand is another tiny skeleton: that of a puppy about five months old.

This is the earliest example we know of man and dog sharing the same grave. There must be many, many later ones.

(From Friends of Man *by Roger Caras. Simon & Schuster, 2001.)*

"YOU MAY BE INTERESTED to know," said Dr. Jafferjee with that clinical detachment which Donald found annoying (though how else could psychiatrists stay sane?) "that Edith's case isn't unique. Ever since the M-Set was discovered in 1980, people have managed to become obsessed with it. Usually they are computer hackers, whose grip on reality is often rather tenuous. There are no less than sixty-three examples of Mandelmania now in the data banks."

"And is there any cure?"

Dr. Jafferjee frowned. "Cure" was a word he seldom used. "Adjustment" was the term he preferred.

"Let's say that in eighty percent of the cases, the subject has been able to resume an—ah—normal life, sometimes with the help of medication or electronic implants. Quite an encouraging figure."

Except, thought Donald, for the twenty percent. Which category does Edith belong to?

For the first week after the tragedy, she had been unnaturally calm; after the funeral, some of their mutual friends had been shocked by her apparent lack of emotion. But Donald knew how badly she had been wounded, and was not surprised when she began to behave irrationally. When she started to wander around the castle at night, searching through the empty rooms and dank passageways that had never been renovated, he realized that it was time to get medical advice.

Nevertheless, he kept putting it off, hoping that Edith would make the normal recovery from the first stages of grief. Indeed, this seemed to be happening. Then Patrick O'Brian died.

Edith's relationship with the old gardener had always been a prickly one, but they had respected each other and shared a mutual love for Ada. The child's death had been as devastating a blow to Pat as to her parents; he also blamed himself for the tragedy. If only he had refused to transplant those cypresses—if only . . .

Pat began drinking heavily again, and was now seldom sober. One cold night, after the landlord of the Black Swan had gently ejected him, he managed to lose his way in the village where he had spent his entire life, and was found frozen to death in the morning. Father McMullen considered that the verdict should have been suicide rather than misadventure; but if it was a sin to give Pat a Christian burial, he would argue that out with God in due course. As, also, the matter of the tiny bundle that Ada held cradled in her arms.

The day after the second funeral, Donald had found Edith sitting in front of a high-resolution monitor, studying one of the infinite miniature versions of the set. She would not speak to him, and presently he realized, to his horror, that she was searching for Ada.

In later years, Donald Craig would often wonder about the relationship that had developed between himself and Jason Bradley. Though they had met only half a dozen times, and then almost always on business, he had felt that bond of mutual sympathy that sometimes grows between two men, and can be almost as strong as a sexual one, even when it has absolutely no erotic content.

Perhaps Donald reminded Bradley of his lost partner Ted Collier, of whom he often spoke. In any event, they enjoyed each other's company, and met even when it was not strictly necessary. Though Kato and the Nippon-Turner syndicate might well have been suspicious, Bradley never compromised his ISA neutrality. Still less did Craig try to exploit it; they might exchange personal secrets, but not professional confidences. Donald never learned what role, if any, Bradley had played in the authority's decision to ban hydrazine.

After Ada's funeral—which Bradley had flown halfway around the world to attend—they had an even closer link. Both had lost a wife and child; though the circumstances were different, the effects were much the same. They became even more intimate, sharing secrets and vulnerabilities that neither had revealed to any other person.

Later, Donald wondered why he did not think of the idea himself; perhaps he was so close to it that he couldn't see the picture for the scan lines.

The fallen cypresses had been cleared away, and the two men were walking by the side of Lake Mandelbrot—for the last time, as it turned out, for both of them—when Bradley outlined the scenario. "It's not *my* idea," he explained, rather apologetically. "I got it from a psychologist friend."

It was a long time before Donald discovered who the "friend" was, but he saw the possibilities at once.

"Do you really think it will work?" he asked.

"That's something you'll have to discuss with Edith's psychiatrist. Even if it *is* a good idea, he may not be willing to go along with it. The NIH syndrome, you know."

"National Institutes of Health?"

"No—Not Invented Here."

Donald laughed, without much humor.

"You're right. But first, I must see if I can do my part. It won't be easy."

That had been an understatement; it was the most difficult task he had ever undertaken in his life. Often he had to stop work, blinded by tears.

And then, in their own mysterious way, the buried circuits of his subconscious triggered a memory that enabled him to continue. Somewhere, years ago, he had come across the story of a surgeon in a third world country who ran an eye-bank which restored sight to poor people. To make a graft possible, corneas had to be removed from the donor within minutes of death.

That surgeon must have had a steady hand, as he sliced into his own mother's eyes. I can do no less, Donald told himself grimly, as he went back to the editing table where he and Edith had spent so many hours together.

Dr. Jafferjee had proved surprisingly receptive. He had asked in a mildly ironic but quite sympathetic manner: "Where did you get the idea? Some pop-psych video-drama?"

"I know it sounds like it. But it seems worth a try—if you approve."

"You've already made the disk?"

"Capsule. I'd like to run it now—I see you've got a hybrid viewer in your outer office."

"Yes. It will even show VHS tapes! I'll call Dolores—I rely on her a good deal." He hesitated, and looked thoughtfully at Donald as if he was going to add something. Instead, he pressed a switch and said softly into the clinic's paging system: "Nurse Dolores—will you please come to my office? Thank you."

Edith Craig is still *somewhere* inside that skull, thought Donald as he sat with Dr. Jafferjee and Nurse Dolores, watching the figure sitting stiffly at the big monitor. Can I smash the invisible yet unyielding barrier that grief has erected, and bring her back to the world of reality?

The familiar black, beetle-shaped image floated on the screen, radiating tendrils that connected it to the rest of the Mandelbrot universe. There was no way of even guessing at the scale, but Donald had already noted the coordinates that defined the size of this particular version. If one could imagine the whole set, stretching out beyond this monitor, it was already larger than the Cosmos that even the Hubble space telescope had yet revealed.

"Are you ready?" asked Dr. Jafferjee.

Donald nodded. Nurse Dolores, sitting immediately behind Edith, glanced toward their camera to indicate that she had heard him.

"Then go ahead."

Donald pressed the EXECUTE key, and the subroutine took over.

The ebon surface of the simulated Lake Mandelbrot seemed to tremble. Edith gave a sudden start of surprise.

"Good!" whispered Dr. Jafferjee. "She's reacting!"

The waters parted. Donald turned away; he could not bear to watch again this latest triumph of his skills. Yet he could still see Ada's image as her voice said gently: "I love you, mother—but you cannot find me here. I exist only in your memories—and I shall always be there. Goodbye. . . ."

Dolores caught Edith's falling body, as the last syllable died away into the irrevocable past.

36.
THE LAST
LUNCH

IT WAS A CHARMING IDEA, though not everyone agreed that it really worked. The decor for the interior of the world's only deep-diving tourist submarine had been borrowed straight from Disney's classic *20,000 Leagues Under the Sea*.

Passengers who boarded the *Piccard* (port of registry, Geneva) found themselves in a plush, though rather oddly proportioned, mid-Victorian drawing room. This was supposed to provide instant reassurance, and divert all thoughts from the several hundred tons pressing on each of the little windows which gave a rather restricted view of the outside world.

The greatest problems that *Piccard*'s builders had had to face were not engineering, but legal ones. Only Lloyd's of London would insure the hull; no one would insure the passengers, who tended to be VIPs with astronomical credit ratings. So before every dive, notarized waivers of liability were collected, as discreetly as possible.

The ritual was only slightly more unsettling than the cabin steward's cheerful litany of possible disasters that passengers on transocean flights had endured for decades. NO SMOKING signs, of course, were no longer necessary; nor did *Piccard* have seat belts and life jackets—which would have been about as useful as parachutes on commercial airliners. Its numerous built-in safety features were unobtrusive and automatic. If worse came to worst, the independent two-man crew capsule would separate from the passenger unit, and each would make a free ascent to the surface, ultrasonic beacons pinging frantically.

This particular dive was the last one of the season: it was getting late in the year, and *Piccard* would soon be airlifted back to calmer seas in the southern hemisphere. Although at the depths the submarine operated, winter and summer made no more difference than day and night, bad weather on the surface could make passengers very, very unhappy.

During the thirty-minute free-fall to the wreck site, *Piccard*'s distinguished guests watched a short video showing the current status of operations, and a map of the planned dive. There was nothing else to see during the descent into darkness, except for the occasional luminous fish attracted to this strange invader of its domain.

Then, abruptly, it seemed that a ghostly dawn was spreading far below. All but the faint red emergency lights in *Piccard* were switched off, as *Titanic*'s prow loomed up ahead.

Almost everyone who saw her now was struck by the same thought: She must have looked much like this, in the Harland and Wolff Shipyard, a hundred years ago. Once again she was surrounded by an elaborate framework of steel scaffolding, while workers swarmed over her. The workers, however, were no longer human.

Visibility was excellent, and the pilot maneuvered *Piccard* so that the passengers on both sides of the cabin could get the best possible view through the narrow portholes. He was extremely careful to avoid the busy robots, who ignored the submarine completely. It was no part of the universe they had been trained to deal with.

"If you look out on the right," said the tour guide—a young Woods Hole graduate, making a little money in his vacation—"you'll see the 'down' cable, stretching up to *Explorer*. And there's a module on the way right now, with its counterweight. Looks like a two-ton unit—

"And there's a robot going to meet it—now the module's unhooked—you see it's got neutral buoyancy, so it can be moved around easily. The robot will carry it over to its attachment point on the lifting cradle, and hook it on. Then the two-ton counterweight that brought it down will be shuttled over to the 'up' cable, and sent back to *Explorer* to be reused. After that's been done ten thousand times, they can lift *Titanic*. This section of her, anyway."

"Sounds a very roundabout way of doing things," commented one of the VIPs. "Why can't they just use compressed air?"

The guide had heard this a dozen times, but had learned to answer all such questions politely. (The pay was good, and so were the fringe benefits.)

"It's possible, ma'am, but much too expensive. The pressure here is *enormous*. I imagine you're all familiar with the standard scuba bottles—they're usually rated at two hundred atmospheres. Well, if you opened one of these down here, the air wouldn't come out. The water would rush *in*—and fill half the bottle!"

Perhaps he'd overdone it; some of the passengers were looking a little worried. So he continued hastily, hoping to divert their thoughts.

"We *do* use some compressed air for trimming and fine control. And in the final stages of the ascent, it will play a major role.

"Now, the skipper is going to fly us toward the stern, along the promenade deck. Then he'll do a reverse run, so you'll all have an equally good view. I won't do any more talking for a while—"

Very slowly, *Piccard* moved the length of the great shadowy hulk. Much of it was in darkness, but some open hatches spilled dramatic fans of light where robots were at work in the interior, fixing buoyancy modules wherever lifting forces could be tolerated.

No one spoke a word as the weed-festooned walls of steel glided by. It was still very hard to grasp the scale of the wreck—still, after a hundred years, one of the largest passenger ships ever built. And the most luxurious, if only for reasons of pure economics. *Titanic* had marked the end of an era; after the war that was coming, no one would ever again be able to afford such opulence. Nor, perhaps, would anyone care to risk it, lest such arrogance once again provoke the envy of the gods.

The mountain of steel faded into the distance; for a while, the nimbus of light surrounding it was still faintly visible. Then there was only the barren seabed drifting below *Piccard*, appearing and disappearing in the twin ovals of its forward lights.

Though it was barren, it was not featureless; it was pitted and gouged, and crisscrossed with trenches and the scars of deep-sea dredges.

"This is the debris field," said the guide, breaking his silence at last. "It was covered with pieces of the ship— crockery, furniture, kitchen utensils, you name it. They were all collected while Lloyd's and the Canadian government were still arguing in the World Court. When the ruling came, it was too late—"

"What's *that*?" one of the passengers suddenly asked. She had caught a glimpse of movement through her little window.

"Where— Let me see— Oh, that's J.J."

"Who?"

"Jason Junior. ISA—sorry, International Seabed Authority's—latest toy. It's being tested out—it's an automatic surveying robot. They hope to have a small fleet of them, so that all the seabeds can be mapped down to one-meter resolution. Then we'll know the ocean as well as we know the Moon. . . ."

Another oasis of light was appearing ahead, and presently resolved itself into a spectacle that was still hard to believe, no matter how many times one had seen it in photos or video displays.

Nothing of the stern portion of the wreck was now visible: it was all buried deep inside the huge, irregular block of ice sitting on the seabed. Protruding out of the ice were dozens of girders, to many of which half-inflated balloons had been attached by cables of varying length.

"It's a *very* tricky job," the young guide said, with obvious admiration. "The big problem is to stop the ice from breaking off and floating up by itself. So there's a lot of internal structure that you can't see. As well as a kind of roof up there on top."

One of the passengers, who obviously hadn't paid attention to the briefing, asked: "Those balloons—didn't you say they couldn't pump air down to this depth?"

"Not enough to lift masses like this. But that's not air. Those flotation bags contain H_2 and O_2—hydrogen and oxygen released by electrolysis. See those cables? They're bringing down millions—no, *billions* of amp-hours from the two nuclear subs four kilometers above us. Enough electricity to run a small township."

He looked at his watch.

"Not so much to see here, I'm afraid. We'll do one circuit in each direction, then start home."

          *   *   *

Piccard dumped its excess weights—they would be collected later—and was sent back along the "up" elevator cable at *Titanic*'s bow. It was time to start autographing the souvenir brochure; and that, to most of the passengers, would be quite a surprise. . . .

D.S.V. "PICCARD"	R.M.S. "TITANIC"
October 14, 2011	April 14, 1912

LUNCHEON

Consommé Fermier	Cockie Leekie

Fillets of Brill
Egg à l'Argenteuil
Chicken à la Maryland
Corned Beef, Vegetables, Dumplings

FROM THE GRILL

Grilled Mutton Chops
Mashed, Fried and Baked Jacket Potatoes

Custard Pudding

Apple Meringue	Pastry

BUFFET

Salmon Mayonnaise	Potted Shrimps
Norwegian Anchovies	Soused Herrings

Plain & Smoked Sardines
Roast Beef
Round of Spiced Beef
Veal & Ham Pie
Virginia & Cumberland Ham

Bologna Sausage	Brawn

Galantine of Chicken
Corned Ox Tongue
Lettuce   Beetroot   Tomatoes

CHEESE

Cheshire, Stilton, Gorgonzola, Edam
Camembert, Roquefort, St. Ivel,
Cheddar

Iced draught Munich Lager Beer 3d. & 6d. a Tankard

"I'm afraid quite a few items are off the menu," said the young guide, in tones of mock apology. "*Piccard's* catering arrangements are rather limited. We don't even run a microwave—would take too much power. So please ignore the grill; I can assure you that the cold buffet is delicious. We also have *some* of the cheeses—but only the milder ones. Gorgonzola didn't seem a very good idea in these confined quarters. . . .

"Oh yes—the lager—it's genuine, straight from Munich! And it cost us rather more than three pence per tankard. Even more than six.

"Enjoy yourselves, ladies and gentlemen. We'll be topside in just one hour."

37.
RESURRECTION

IT HAD NOT BEEN EASY to arrange, and had taken months of arguing across the border. However, the joint funeral services had gone smoothly enough; for once, sharing the same tragedy, Christian could talk politely to Christian. The fact that one of the dead had come from Northern Ireland helped a good deal; coffins could be lowered into the ground simultaneously in Dublin and Belfast.

As the "Lux aeterna" of Verdi's *Requiem Mass* ebbed softly away, Edith Craig turned to Dolores and asked: "Should I tell Dr. Jafferjee now? Or will he think I'm crazy again?"

Dolores frowned, then answered in that lilting Caribbean accent that had once helped to reach the far place where Edith's mind was hiding:

"Please, dear, *don't* use that word. And yes, I think you should. It's about time we spoke to him again—he'll be getting worried. He's not like some doctors I could mention—he keeps track of his patients. They're not just case numbers to him."

Dr. Jafferjee was indeed pleased to receive Edith's call; he wondered where it was coming from, but she did not enlighten him. He could see that she was sitting in a large room with cane furniture (ah, probably the tropics—Dolores' home island?) and was happy to note that she seemed completely relaxed. There were two large photographs on the wall behind her, and he recognized both—Ada, and "Colleen."

Physician and ex-patient greeted each other with warmth; then Edith said, a little nervously: "You may think I'm starting on another hopeless quest—and you may be right. But at least *this* time I know what I'm doing—and I'll be working with some of the world's top scientists. The odds may be a million to one against success. But that's infinitely—and I *mean* infinitely—better than . . . than . . . finding what you need in the M-Set."

Not what you need, thought Dr. Jafferjee: what you *want*. But he merely said, rather cautiously: "Go ahead, Edith. I'm intrigued—and completely in the dark."

"What do you know about cryonics?"

"Not much. I know a lot of people have been frozen, but it's never been proved that they can be— Oh! I see what you're driving at! What a fantastic idea!"

"But not a ridiculous one?"

"Well, your million-to-one odds may be optimistic. But for such a payoff—no, I wouldn't say it was ridiculous. And if you're worried that I'll ask Dolores to put you on the first plane back to the clinic, you needn't be. Even if your project doesn't succeed, it could be the best possible therapy."

But only if, Jafferjee thought, you aren't overwhelmed by the almost inevitable failure. Still, that would be years ahead. . . .

"I'm so glad you feel that way. As soon as I heard that they were going to keep Colleen in the hope of identifying her, I *knew* what I had to do. I don't believe in destiny—or fate—but how could I possibly turn down the chance?"

How could you, indeed? thought Jafferjee. You have lost

one daughter; you hope to gain another. A Sleeping Beauty, to be awakened not by a young prince, but an aging princess. No—a witch—a good one, this time!—possessing powers utterly beyond the dreams of any Irish lass born in the Nineteenth Century.

If—*if!*—it works, what a strange new world Colleen will face! *She* would be the one to need careful psychological counseling. But this was all the wildest extrapolation.

"I don't wish to pour cold water on the idea," Jafferjee said. "But surely, even if you can revive the body—won't there be irreversible brain damage after a hundred years?"

"That's exactly what I was afraid of, when I started thinking about it. But there's a great deal of research that makes it very plausible—I've been quite surprised. More than that—impressed. Have you ever heard of Professor Ralph Merkle?"

"Vaguely."

"More than thirty years ago, he and a couple of other young mathematicians revolutionized cryptography by inventing the public-key system—I won't bother to explain that, but it made every cipher machine in the world, and a lot of spy networks, obsolete overnight.

"Then, in 1990—sorry, 1989—he published a classic paper called 'Molecular Repair of the Brain'—"

"Oh, *that* fellow!"

"Good—I was sure you must have heard of his work. He pointed out that even if there had been gross damage to the brain, it could be repaired by the molecule-sized machines he was quite certain would be invented in the next century. *Now.*"

"And have they been?"

"Many of them. Look at the computer-controlled micro-subs the surgeons are using now, to ream out the arteries of stroke victims. You can't watch a science channel these days without seeing the latest achievements of nanotechnology."

"But to repair a whole brain, molecule by molecule! Think of the sheer numbers involved!"

"About ten to the twenty-third. A trivial number."

"Indeed." Jafferjee was not quite sure whether Edith was joking; no—she was perfectly serious.

"Very well. Suppose you *do* repair a brain, right down to the last detail. Would that bring the person back to life? Complete with memories? Emotions? And everything else— whatever it is—that makes a specific, self-conscious individual?"

"Can you give me a good reason why it wouldn't? I don't believe the brain is any more mysterious than the rest of the body—and we know how *that* works, in principle if not in detail. Anyway, there's only one way to find out—and we'll learn a lot in the process."

"How long do you think it will take?"

"Ask me in five years. Then I may know if we'll need another decade—or a century. Or forever."

"I can only wish you luck. It's a fascinating project—and you're going to have lots of problems beside the purely technical ones. Her relations, for example, if they're ever located."

"It doesn't seem likely. The latest theory is that she was a stowaway, and so not on the passenger list."

"Well, the church. The media. Thousands of sponsors. Ghost writers who want to do her autobiography. I'm beginning to feel sorry for that poor girl already."

And he could not help thinking, though he did not say it aloud: I hope Dolores won't be jealous.

Donald, of course, had been both astonished and indignant: husbands (and wives) always were on such occasions.

"She didn't even leave any message?" he said unbelievingly. Dr. Jafferjee shook his head.

"There's no need to worry. She'll contact you as soon as

she's settled down. It will take her a while to adjust. Give her a few weeks."

"Do you know where she's gone?"

The doctor did not answer, which was answer enough.

"Well, are you quite sure she's safe?"

"No doubt of it; she's in extremely good hands." The psychiatrist made one of those lengthy pauses which were part of his stock-in-trade.

"You know, Mr. Craig, I should be quite annoyed with you."

"Why?" asked Donald, frankly astonished.

"You've cost me the best member of my staff—my right-hand woman."

"Nurse Dolores? I wondered why I'd not seen her—I wanted to thank her for all she'd done."

Another of those calculated pauses; then Dr. Jafferjee said: "She's helped Edith more than you imagine. Obviously, you've never guessed, and this may be a shock to you. But I owe you the truth—it will help you with your own adjustment.

"Edith's prime orientation isn't toward men—and Dolores actively disliked them, though she was sometimes kind enough to make an exception in my case. . . .

"She was able to contact Edith on the physical level even before we connected on the mental one. They will be very good for each other. But I'll miss her, dammit."

Donald Craig was speechless for a moment. Then he blurted out: "You mean—they were having an affair? And you *knew* it?"

"Of course I did; my job as a physician is to help my patients in any way I can. You're an intelligent man, Mr. Craig—I'm surprised that seems to shock you."

"Surely it's . . . *unprofessional* conduct!"

"What nonsense! Just the reverse—it's highly professional.

Oh, back in the barbarous Twentieth Century many people would have agreed with you. Can you believe it was a *crime* in those days for the staff of institutions to have any kind of sex with patients under their care, even though that would often have been the best possible therapy for them?

"One good thing did come out of the AIDS epidemic—it forced people to be honest: it wiped out the last remnants of the Puritan aberration. My Hindu colleagues—with their temple prostitutes and erotic sculpture—had the right idea all the time. Too bad it took the West three thousand years of misery to catch up with them."

Dr. Jafferjee paused for breath, giving Donald Craig time to marshal his own thoughts. He could not help feeling that the doctor had lost some of his professional detachment. Had he been erotically interested in the inaccessible Nurse Dolores? Or did he have deeper problems?

But, of course, everyone knew just why people became psychiatrists in the first place. . . .

With luck, you could cure yourself. And even if you failed, the work was interesting—and the pay was excellent.

FINALE

38.
RICHTER
EIGHT

JASON BRADLEY WAS on the bridge of *Glomar Explorer*, monitoring J.J.'s progress on the seabed, when he felt the sudden sharp hammerblow. The two electronics technicians watching the displays never even noticed; they probably thought it was some change in the incessant rhythm of the ship's machinery. Yet for a chilling instant Jason was reminded of a moment almost a century ago, equally unnoticed by most of the passengers. . . .

But, of course, *Explorer* was at anchor (in four kilometers of water, and how *that* would have astonished Captain Smith!) and no iceberg could possibly creep undetected through her radar. Nor, at drifting speed, would it do much worse than scrape off a little paint.

Before Jason could even call the communications center, a red star began to flash on the satfax screen. In addition, a piercing audio alarm, guaranteed to set teeth on edge as it warbled up and down through a kilocycle range, sounded on the unit's seldom-used speaker. Jason punched the audio cutoff, and concentrated on the message. Even the two landlubbers beside him now realized that *something* was wrong.

"What is it?" one of them asked anxiously.

"Earthquake—and a big one. Must have been close."

"Any danger?"

"Not to *us*. I wonder where the epicenter is. . . ."

Bradley had to wait a few minutes for the seismograph-computer networks to do their calculations. Then a message appeared on the fax screen:

> SUBSEA EARTHQUAKE ESTIMATED RICHTER 7
> EPICENTER APPROX 55 W 44 N.
> ALERT ALL ISLANDS AND COASTAL AREAS
> NORTH ATLANTIC

Nothing else happened for a few seconds; then another line appeared:

> CORRECTION: UPDATE TO RICHTER 8

Four kilometers below, J.J. was patiently and efficiently going about its business, gliding over the seabed at an altitude of ten meters and a speed of a comfortable eight knots. (Some nautical traditions refused to die; knots and fathoms still survived into the metric age.) Its navigation program had been set so that it scanned overlapping swaths, like a plowman driving back and forth across a field being prepared for the next harvest.

The first shock wave bothered J.J. no more than it had the *Explorer*. Even the two nuclear submarines had been completely unaffected; they had been designed to withstand far worse—though their commanders had spent a few anxious seconds speculating about depth charges.

J.J. continued its automatic quest, collecting and recording megabytes of information every second. Ninety-nine percent of this would never be of the slightest interest to anyone—and it might be centuries before scientific gold was found in the residue.

To eye or video camera, the seabed here appeared almost completely featureless, but it had been chosen with care. The original "debris field" around the severed stern section had long ago been cleared of all interesting items; even the lumps of coal spilled from the bunkers had been salvaged and made into souvenirs. However, only two years ago a magnetometer search had revealed anomalies near the bow which might be worth investigating. J.J. was just the entity for the job; in another few hours it would have completed the survey, and would return to its floating base.

"It looks like 1929 all over again," said Bradley.

Back in the ISA lab, Dr. Zwicker shook his head.

"No—much worse, I'm afraid."

In Tokyo, at another node of the hastily arranged conference, Kato asked: "What happened in 1929?"

"The Grand Banks earthquake. It triggered a turbidity current—call it an underwater avalanche. Snapped the telegraph cables one after the other, like cotton, as it raced across the seabed. That's how its speed was calculated—sixty kilometers an hour. Perhaps more."

"Then it could reach us in—my God—three or four hours. What's the likelihood of damage?"

"Impossible to say at this stage. Best case—very little. The 1929 quake didn't touch *Titanic,* though many people thought she'd been buried; luckily, it was a couple of hundred kilometers to the west. Most of the sediment was diverted into a canyon, and missed the wreck completely."

"Excuse me," interrupted Rupert Parkinson, from his London office. "We've just heard that one of our flotation modules has surfaced. Jumped twenty meters out of the water. And we've lost telemetry to the wreck. How about you, Kato?"

Kato hesitated only a moment; then he called out something in Japanese to an associate off-screen.

"I'll check with *Peter* and *Maury*. Dr. Zwicker—what's your worst-case analysis?"

"Our first quick look suggests a few meters of sediment. We'll have a better computer modeling within the hour."

"A meter wouldn't be too bad."

"It could wreck our schedule, dammit."

"A report from *Maury*, gentlemen," said Kato. "No problem—everything normal."

"But for how long? If that . . . avalanche . . . really is racing toward us, we should pull up whatever equipment we can. What do *you* advise, Dr. Zwicker?"

The scientist was just about to speak when Bradley whispered urgently in his ear. Zwicker looked startled, then glum—then nodded in reluctant agreement.

"I don't think I should say any more, gentlemen. Mr. Bradley is more experienced in this area than I am. Before I give any *specific* advice, I should consult our legal department."

There was a shocked silence; then Rupert Parkinson said quickly: "We're all men of the world; we can understand that ISA doesn't want to get involved in lawsuits. So let's not waste time. We're pulling up what we can. And I advise you to do the same, Kato—just in case Dr. Zwicker's *worst* case is merely the bad one."

That was precisely what the scientist had feared. A submarine seaquake was impressive enough; but—as a fission bomb serves as detonator for a fusion one—it might merely act as a trigger to release even greater forces.

Millions of years of solar energy had been stored in the petrochemicals beneath the bed of the Atlantic; barely a century's worth had been tapped by man.

The rest was still waiting.

39.
PRODIGAL
SON

ON THE BED of the Atlantic, a billion dollars' worth of robots downed tools and started to float up to the surface. There was no great hurry; no lives were at stake, even though fortunes were. *Titanic* shares were already plunging on the world's stock exchanges, giving media humorists an opportunity for all-too-obvious jokes.

The great offshore oil fields were also playing it safe. Although Hibernia and Avalon, in relatively shallow water, had little to fear from turbidity currents, they had suspended all operations, and were doubly and triply checking their emergency and backup systems. Now there was nothing to do but to wait—and to admire the superb auroral displays that had already made this sunspot cycle the most spectacular ever recorded.

Just before midnight—no one was getting much sleep—Bradley was standing on *Explorer*'s helicopter pad, watching the great curtains of ruby and emerald fire being drawn across the northern sky. He was not a member of the crew; if the skipper or anyone else wanted him, he would be available in seconds.

Busy people, especially in emergencies, did not care to have
observers standing behind their backs—however well inten-
tioned or highly qualified they might be.

And the summons, when it did come, was not from the
bridge, but the operations center.

"Jason? Ops here. We have a problem. J.J. won't acknowledge our recall signal."

Bradley felt a curious mix of emotions. First there was
concern at losing one of the lab's most promising—and
expensive—pieces of equipment. Then there was the inevitable
mental question mark—"What could have gone wrong?"—
followed immediately by: "What can we do about it?"

But there was also something deeper. J.J. represented an
enormous personal investment of time, effort, thought . . . even
devotion. He recalled all those jokes about the robot's paternity;
there was some truth in them. Creating a real son (what had
happened to the flesh-and-blood J.J.?) had required very much less
energy. . . .

Hell, Jason told himself, it's only a machine! It could be
rebuilt; we still have all the programs. Nothing would be lost
except the information collected on the present mission.

No—a great deal would be lost. It was even possible that
the whole project might be abandoned; developing J.J. had
stretched ISA's funding and resources to the limit. At the very
least, Operation NEPTUNE would be delayed for years—
probably beyond Zwicker's lifetime. The scientist was a prickly
old S.O.B., but Jason liked and admired him. Losing J.J. would
break his heart. . . .

Even as he hurried toward the ops center, Bradley was
collecting and analyzing reports over his wristcom.

"You're sure J.J.'s operating normally?"

"Yes—beacon's working fine—last housekeeping report

fifteen minutes ago said all systems nominal—continuing with search pattern. But it just won't respond to the recall signal."

"Damn! The lab told me that algorithm had been fixed. Just keep trying. . . . Boost your power as much as you can. What's the latest on the quake?"

"Bad—Mount Pelée is rumbling—they're evacuating Martinique. And tsunami warnings have been sent out all over, of course."

"But what about the Grand Banks? Any sign of that avalanche starting yet?"

"The seismographs are all jangling—no one's quite sure what the hell's happening. Just a minute while I get an update—

"—ah, here's something. The Navy antisubmarine network—didn't know it was still running!—is getting chopped up. So are the Atlantic cables—just like '29. . . . Yes—it's heading this way."

"How long before it hits us?"

"If it doesn't run out of steam, a good three hours. Maybe four."

Time enough, thought Bradley. He knew exactly what he had to do.

"Moon pool?" he called. "Open up Deep Jeep. I'm going down."

I'm really enjoying this, Bradley told himself. For the first time, I have an ironclad excuse to take Deep Jeep down to the wreck, without having to make application through channels, in triplicate. There'll be plenty of time later to do the paperwork—or to input the electronic memos. . . .

To speed the descent, Deep Jeep was heavily overweighted; this was no time to worry about littering the seabed with discarded ballast. Only twenty minutes after the brilliant auroral glow had faded in the waters above him, Bradley saw the first phosphorescent nimbus around *Titanic*'s prow. He did not need it, of course, because he knew his exact location, and the wreck was not even his target; but he was glad that the lights had been switched on again for his exclusive benefit.

J.J. was only half a kilometer away, going about its business with simpleminded concentration and devotion to duty. The monotonous *ping . . . ping-ping* call sign of its beacon filled Deep Jeep's tiny bubble of air every ten seconds, and it was also clearly visible on the search sonar.

Without much hope, Bradley retransmitted the emergency recall sequence, and continued to do so as he approached the recalcitrant robot. He was not surprised, or disappointed, at the total lack of response. Not to worry, he told himself; I've lots of other tricks up my sleeve.

He saved the next one until they were only ten meters apart. Deep Jeep could easily outrun J.J., and Bradley had no difficulty in placing his vehicle athwart the robot's precomputed track. Such underwater confrontations had often been arranged, to test J.J.'s obstacle avoidance algorithms—and these, at least, now operated exactly as planned.

J.J. came to a complete halt, and surveyed the situation. At this point-blank range Bradley could just detect, with his unaided ears, a piccololike subharmonic as the robot scanned the obstacle ahead, and tried to identify it.

He took this opportunity of sending out the recall command once more; no luck. It was pointless to try again; the problem must be in the software.

J.J. turned ninety degrees left, and headed off at right angles to its original course. It went only ten meters, then swung back to its old bearing, hoping to avoid the obstruction. But Bradley was there already.

While J.J. was thinking this over, Bradley tried a new gambit. He switched on the external sound transducer.

"J.J.," he said. "Can you hear me?"

"Yes," the robot answered promptly.

"Do you recognize me?"

"Yes, Mr. Bradley."

Good, thought Bradley. We're getting somewhere. . . .

"Do you have any problems?"

"No. All systems are normal."

"We have sent you a recall—Subprogram 999. Have you received it?"

"No. I have not received it."

Well, thought Bradley, whatever science fiction writers may have pretended, robots won't lie—unless they're programmed to do so. And no one's played that dirty trick on J.J.—I hope. . . .

"One has been sent out. I repeat: Obey Code 999. Acknowledge."

"I acknowledge."

"Then execute."

"Command not understood."

Damn. We're going around in circles, Bradley realized. And we could do that, literally, until we both run out of power—or patience.

While Bradley was considering his next step, *Explorer* interrupted the dialogue.

"Deep Jeep—sorry you're having no luck so far. But we've an update for you—and a message from the Prof."

"Go ahead."

"You're missing some real fireworks. There's been a—well, *blowout's* the only word—around forty west, fifty north. Much too deep to do any serious damage to the offshore rigs, luckily—but hydrocarbon gas is bubbling up by the millions of cubic meters. *And it's ignited*—we can see the glare from here—forget the aurora! You should see the Earthsat images: looks as if the North Atlantic's on fire."

I'm sure it's very spectacular, thought Bradley. But how does it affect *me*?

"What's that about a message from Dr. Zwicker?"

"He asked us to tell you Tommy Gold was right. Said you'd understand."

"Frankly, I'm not interested in proving scientific theories at the moment. How long before I must come up?"

Bradley felt no sense of alarm—only of urgency. He could drop his remaining ballast and blow his tanks in a matter of seconds, and be safely on his way up long before any submarine avalanche could overwhelm him. But he was determined to complete his mission, for reasons which were now as much personal as professional.

"Latest estimate is one hour—you may have more. Plenty of time before it gets here—if it does."

An hour was ample; five minutes might be enough.

"J.J.," he commanded. "I am giving you a new program. Command Five Two Seven."

That was main power cutoff, which should leave only the backup systems running. Then J.J. would have no choice but to surface.

"Command Five Two Seven accepted."

Good—it had worked! J.J.'s external lights flickered, and the little attitude-control propellers idled to a halt. For a moment, J.J. was dead in the water. Hope I haven't overdone it, Bradley thought.

Then the lights came on again, and the props started to spin once more.

Well, it was a nice try. Nothing had gone wrong this time, but it was impossible to remember everything, in a system as complex as J.J.'s. Bradley had simply forgotten one small detail.

Some commands only worked in the lab; they were disabled on operational missions. The override had been automatically overridden.

That left only one option. If gentle persuasion had failed, he would have to use brute force. Deep Jeep was much stronger than J.J.—which in any case had no limbs with which to defend itself. Any wrestling match would be very one-sided.

But it would also be undignified. There was a better way.

Bradley put Deep Jeep into reverse, so that the submersible no longer blocked J.J. The robot considered the new situation for a few seconds, then set off again on its rounds. Such dedication was indeed admirable, but it could be overdone. Was it true that archaeologists had found a Roman sentry still at his post in Pompeii, overwhelmed by the ashes of Vesuvius because no officer had come to relieve him of his duty? That was very much what J.J. now seemed determined to do.

"Sorry about this," Bradley muttered as he caught up with the unsuspecting machine.

He jammed Deep Jeep's manipulator arm into the main prop, and pieces of metal flew off in all directions. The auxiliary fans spun J.J. in a half circle, then slowed to rest.

There was only one way out of this situation, and J.J. did not stop to argue.

The intermittent beacon signal switched over to the continuous distress call—the robot Mayday—which meant "Come and get me!"

Like a bomber dropping its payload, J.J. released the iron ballast weight which gave it neutral buoyancy, and started its swift rise to the surface.

"J.J.'s on the way up," Bradley reported to *Explorer.* "Should be there in twenty minutes."

Now the robot was safe; it would be tracked by half a

dozen systems as soon as it broke water, and would be back in the moon pool well before Deep Jeep.

"I hope you realize," Bradley muttered as J.J. disappeared into the liquid sky above, "that hurt me much more than it hurt you."

40.

TOUR OF
INSPECTION

JASON BRADLEY WAS just preparing to drop his own ballast and follow J.J. up to the surface when *Explorer* called again.

"Nice work, Jason—we're tracking J.J. on the way up. The inflatables are already waiting for him.

"But don't drop your weights yet. There's a small job the N-T group would like you to do—it will only take a minute or five."

"Do I have that long?"

"No problem, or we wouldn't ask. A good forty minutes before the thing hits—it looks like a weather front on our computer simulations. We'll give you plenty of warning."

Bradley considered the situation. Deep Jeep could easily reach the Nippon-Turner site within five minutes, and he would like to have one last look at *Titanic*—both sections, if possible. There was no risk; even if the arrival estimate was wildly in error, he would still have several minutes of warning time and could be a thousand meters up before the avalanche swept past below.

241

"What do they want me to do?" he asked, swinging Deep Jeep around so that the ice-shrouded stern was directly ahead on his sonar scan.

"*Maury* has a problem with its power cables—can't haul them up. May be snagged somewhere. Can you check?"

"Will do."

It was a reasonable request, since he was virtually on the spot. The massive, neutral-buoyancy conductors which had carried down their enormous amperages to the wreck cost millions of dollars; no wonder the submarines were trying to winch them up. He assumed that *Peter the Great* had already succeeded.

He had only Deep Jeep's own lights to illuminate the ice mountain still tethered to the seabed, awaiting a moment of release that now might never come. Moving cautiously, to avoid the wires linking it with the straining oxy-hydrogen balloons, he skirted the mass until he came to the pair of thick power cables running up to the submarine far above.

"Can't see anything wrong," he said. "Just give another good pull."

Only seconds later, the great cables vibrated majestically, like the strings of some gigantic musical instrument. It seemed to Bradley that he should feel the wave of infrasound spreading out from them.

But the cables remained defiantly taut.

"Sorry," he said. "Nothing I can do. Maybe the shock wave jammed the release mechanism."

"That's the feeling up here. Well, many thanks. Better come home—you've still plenty of time, but the latest estimate is that half a billion tons of mud is heading your way. They say it's like the Mississippi in full spate."

"How many minutes before it gets here?"

"Twenty—no, fifteen."

I'd like to visit the prow, Bradley thought wistfully, but I won't press my luck. Even if I do miss the chance of being the very last man ever to set eyes on *Titanic.*

Reluctantly, he jettisoned Number 1 ballast weight, and Deep Jeep started to rise. He had one final glimpse of the immense ice-encrusted framework as he lifted away from it; then he concentrated on the pair of cables glimmering in his forward lights. Just as the anchor chain of his boat gives reassurance to a scuba diver, they also provided Bradley with a welcoming link to the world far above.

He was just about to drop the second weight, and increase his rate of ascent, when things started to go wrong.

Maury was still hopefully jerking on the cables, trying to retrieve its expensive hardware, when something finally gave way. But not, unfortunately, what was intended.

There was a loud *ping* from the anticollision sonar, then a crash that shook Deep Jeep and threw Bradley against his seat belt. He had a brief glimpse of a huge white mass soaring past him, and up into the heights above.

Deep Jeep started to sink. Bradley dropped the remaining two ballast weights.

His rate of descent dropped, almost to zero. But not quite; he was still sinking, very slowly, toward the seabed.

Bradley sat in silence for a few minutes. Then, despite himself, he began to laugh. He was in no immediate danger, and it really *was* quite funny.

"*Explorer,*" he said. "You're not going to believe this. I've just been hit by an iceberg."

41.
FREE
ASCENT

EVEN NOW, BRADLEY did not consider himself to be in real jeopardy; he was more annoyed than alarmed. Yet on the face of it, the situation seemed dramatic enough. He was stranded on the seabed, his buoyancy lost. The glancing blow from the ascending mini-iceberg must have sheared away some of Deep Jeep's flotation modules. And as if that were not enough, the biggest underwater avalanche ever recorded was bearing down upon him, and now due to arrive in ten or fifteen minutes. He could not help feeling like a character in an old Steven Spielberg movie.

First step, he thought: see if Deep Jeep's propulsion system can provide enough lift to get me out of this. . . .

The submarine stirred briefly, and blasted up a cloud of mud which filled the surrounding water with a dazzling cloud of reflected light. Deep Jeep rose a few meters, then settled back. The batteries would be flat long before he could reach the surface.

I hate to do this, he told himself. A couple of million bucks down the drain—or at least on the seabed. But maybe we can salvage the rest of Deep Jeep when this is all over—just as they did with good old *Alvin*, long ago.

Bradley reached for the "chicken switch," and unlatched the protective cover.

"Deep Jeep calling *Explorer*. I've got to make a free ascent; you won't hear from me until I reach the surface. Keep a good sonar lookout—I'll be coming up fast. Get your thrusters started, in case you have to sidestep me."

Calculations had shown—and tests had confirmed—that shorn of its surrounding equipment Deep Jeep's buoyant life-support sphere would hit forty klicks, and jump high enough out of the water to land on the deck of any ship that was too close. Or, of course, hole it below the water line, if it was unlucky enough to score a direct hit.

"We're ready, Jason. Good luck."

He turned the little red key, and the lights flickered once as the heavy current pulsed through the detonators.

There are some engineering systems which can never be fully checked out, before the time when they are needed. Deep Jeep had been well designed, but testing the escape mechanism at four hundred atmospheres pressure would have required most of ISA's budget.

The twin explosive charges separated the buoyant life-support sphere from the rest of the vehicle, exactly as planned.

But, as Jason had often said, the sea could always think of something else. The titanium hull was already stressed to its maximum safe value; and the shock waves, relatively feeble though they were, converged and met at the same spot.

It was too late for fear or regret; in the fraction of a second that was left to him before the sphere imploded, Jason Bradley had time for only a single thought: This is a good place to die.

42.
THE VILLA,
AT SUNSET

AS HE DROVE his hired car past the elaborate iron gates, the beautifully manicured trees and flowerbeds triggered a momentary flashback. With a deliberate effort of will, Donald Craig forced down the upwelling memories of Conroy Castle. He would never see it again; that chapter of his life was over.

The sadness was still there, and part of it would always be with him. And yet he also felt a sense of liberation; it was not too late—what was Milton's most misquoted phrase?—to seek fresh woods and pastures new. I'm trying to reprogram myself, Donald thought wryly. Open new file. . . .

There was a parking space waiting for him a few meters from the elegant Georgian house; he locked the hired car, and walked to the front door. There was a very new brass plate at eye level, just above the bell push and speaker grill. Though Donald could not see any camera lens, he did not doubt that one was observing him.

The plate carried a single line, in bold lettering:

Dr. Evelyn Merrick, Ph.D. (Psych)

Donald looked at it thoughtfully for a few seconds, then smiled and reached for the bell push. But the door anticipated him.

There was a faint click as it swung open; then Dame Eva said, in that probing yet sympathetic voice that would often remind him of Dr. Jafferjee: "Welcome aboard, Mr. Craig. Any friend of Jason's is a friend of mine."

43.
EXORCISM

2012 April 15, 2:00 A.M.

It was a bad time for the media networks—too early for the Americas, not late enough for the evening Euronews. In any case, it was a story that had peaked; few were now interested in a race that had been so well and truly lost.

Every year, for a century now, the U.S. Coast Guard had dropped a wreath at this same spot. But *this* centennial was a very special one: the focus of so many vanished hopes and dreams—and fortunes.

Glomar Explorer had been swung into the wind, so that her forward deckhouse gave her distinguished guests some protection from the icy gusts from the north. Yet it was not as cold as it had been on that immaculate night a hundred years ago, when the whole North Atlantic had lain all Danaë to the stars.

There was no one aboard who had been present the last time *Explorer* had paid its tribute to the dead, but many must have recalled that secret ceremony on the other side of the world, in a bloodstained century that now seemed to belong to another age. The human race had matured a little, but still had far to go before it could claim to be civilized.

The slow movement of Elgar's Second Symphony ebbed into silence. No music could have been more appropriate than this haunting farewell to the Edwardian Era, composed during the very years that *Titanic* grew in the Belfast shipyard.

All eyes were on the tall, gray-haired man who picked up the single wreath and dropped it gently over the side. For a long time he stood in silence; though all his companions on the windswept deck could share his emotions, for some they were especially poignant. They had been with him aboard the *Knorr,* when the TV monitor had shown the first wreckage on the morning of 1 September 1985. And there was one whose dead wife's wedding ring had been cast into these same waters, a quarter of a century ago.

This time, *Titanic* was lost forever to the race that had conceived and built her; no human eyes would look upon her scattered fragments again.

More than a few men were free at last, from the obsessions of a lifetime.

44.
EPILOGUE:
THE DEEPS
OF TIME

THE STAR ONCE called the Sun had changed little since the far-off days when men had worshiped it.

Two planets had gone—one by design, one by accident—and Saturn's rings had lost much of their glory. But on the whole, the Solar System had not been badly damaged during its brief occupancy by a space-faring species.

Indeed, some regions still showed signs of past improvements. The Martian oceans had dwindled to a few shallow lakes, but the great forests of mutated pines still survived along the equatorial belt. For ages to come, they would maintain and protect the ecology they had been designed to create.

Venus—once called New Eden—had reverted to its former Hell. And of Mercury, nothing remained. The system's mother lode of heavy metals had been whittled away through millennia of astroengineering. The last remnant of the core—with its unexpected and providential bonus of magnetic monopoles—had been used to build the worldships of the Exodus Fleet.

And Pluto, of course, had been swallowed by the fearsome singularity which the best scientists of the human race were still vainly struggling to comprehend, even as they fled in search of safer suns. There was no trace of this ancient tragedy, when the Seeker fell earthward out of deep space, following an invisible trail.

The interstellar probe that Man had launched toward the Galactic core had reconnoitered a dozen stars before its signals had been intercepted by another civilization. The Seeker knew, to within a few dozen light-years, the origin of the primitive machine whose trajectory it was retracing. It had explored almost a hundred solar systems, and had discovered much. The planet it was approaching now was little different from many others it had inspected; there was no cause for excitement, even if the Seeker had been capable of such an emotion.

The radio spectrum was silent, except for the hiss and crash of the cosmic background. There were none of the glittering networks which covered the nightlands of most technologically developed worlds. Nor, when it entered atmosphere, did the Seeker find the chemical traces of industrial development.

Automatically, it went into the standard search routine. It dissolved into a million components, which scattered over the face of the planet. Some would never return, but would merely send back information. No matter; the Seeker could always create others to replace them. Only its central core was indispensable—and there were backup copies of that, safely stored at right angles to all three dimensions of normal space.

Earth had orbited the sun only a few times before the Seeker had gathered all the easily accessible information about the abandoned planet. It was little enough; megayears of winds and rains had wiped away all man's cities, and the slow grinding of the tectonic plates had completely changed the patterns of land and sea. Continents had become oceans; seabeds had become plains, which had then been wrinkled into mountains. . . .

. . . The anomaly was the faintest of echoes on a neutrino scan, but it attracted immediate attention. Nature abhorred straight lines, right angles, repeated patterns—except on the scale of crystals and snowflakes. This was millions of times larger; indeed, it dwarfed the Seeker. It could only be the work of intelligence.

The object lay in the heart of a mountain, beneath kilometers of sedimentary rock. To reach it would require only seconds; to excavate it without doing any damage, and to learn all its secrets, might require months or years.

The scan was repeated, at higher resolution. Now it was observed that the object was made from ferrous alloys of an extremely simple type. No civilization that could build an interstellar probe would have used such crude materials. The Seeker almost felt disappointment. . . .

Yet, primitive though this object was, no other artifact of comparable size or complexity had been found. It might, after all, be worth the trouble of recovering.

The Seeker's high-level systems considered the problem for many, many microseconds, analyzing all the possibilities that might arise. Presently the Master Correlator made its decision.

"Let us begin."

SOURCES
AND
ACKNOWLEDG-
MENTS

R.M.S. *TITANIC* HAS HAUNTED me all my life, as is amply demonstrated by this extract from *Arthur C. Clarke's Chronicles of the Strange and Mysterious* (Collins, 1987):

"My very first attempt at a full-length science-fiction story (fortunately long since destroyed) concerned that typical disaster of the spaceways, the collision between an interplanetary liner and a large meteorite—or small comet, if you prefer. I was quite proud of the title, *Icebergs of Space*—never dreaming at the time that such things really existed. I have always been a little too fond of surprise endings. In the last line I revealed the name of the wrecked spaceship. It was—wait for it—*Titanic*."

More than four decades later, I returned to the subject in *Imperial Earth* (1976), bringing the wreck to New York to celebrate the 2276 Quincentennial. At the time of writing, of course, no one knew that the ship was in two badly damaged portions.

Meanwhile I had grown to know Bill MacQuitty, the Irish movie maker (and much else) to whom this book is dedicated. Following the success of his superb *A Night to Remember* (1958), Bill was determined to film my 1961 novel *A Fall of Moondust*; however, the Rank Organization refused to dabble in fantasy (men on the Moon, indeed!) and the project was turned down. I am happy to say that the novel is now being turned into a TV mini-series by another close friend, Michael Deakin. If you wonder how we manage to find seas of dust on the moon, stay tuned.

I am also indebted to Bill MacQuitty for photographs, plans, drawings, and documents on R.M.S. *Titanic*—especially the menu reproduced in Chapter 36, "The Last Lunch." Bill's beautiful book *Irish Gardens* (text by Edward Hyams; Macdonald, London, 1967) also provided much inspiration.

It is pleasant to record that Bill's director of photography was Geoffrey Unsworth—who, a decade later, also filmed *2001: A Space Odyssey*. I can still remember Geoffrey wandering round the set with a slightly bemused expression, telling all and sundry: "I've been in this business for forty years—and Stanley's just taught me something I didn't know." Michael Crichton has reminded me that *Superman* was dedicated to Geoffrey, who died during its production, much mourned by all those who had worked with him.

This novel would not have been possible, of course, without inputs from the two classic books on the subject, Walter Lord's *A Night To Remember* (Allen Lane, 1976) and Robert Ballard's *The Discovery of the Titanic* (Madison Press Books, 1987), both of which are beyond praise. Two other books I have also found very valuable are Walter Lord's recent "sequel" *The*

Night Lives On (William Morrow, 1986) and Charles Pellegrino's *Her Name, Titanic* (Avon, 1990). I am also extremely grateful to Charlie (who appears in Chapter 43) for a vast amount of technical information about "Bringing up Baby"—an enterprise which we both regard with very mixed feelings.

Martin Gardner's book *The Wreck of the Titanic Foretold?* (Prometheus Books, 1986) reprints the extraordinary Morgan Robertson novel, *The Wreck of the Titan* (1898!), which Lord Aldiss refers to in Chapter 9. Martin makes a good case for intelligent anticipation on Robertson's part; nevertheless, I cannot blame anyone who thinks there must have been *some* feedback from 1912. . . .

Since many of the events in this novel have already occurred—or are about to do so—it has often been necessary to refer to real individuals. I hope they will enjoy my occasional extrapolation of their activities.

"The Century Syndrome" (Chapter 4) already has many people worried, though we will have to wait until 1/1/00 to see whether matters are as bad as I suggest. While I was writing this book, my most long-standing American friend, Dr. Charles Fowler (GCA, 1942—though neither of us can quite believe it), sent me an article from the *Boston Globe* entitled "Mainframes have a problem with the year 2000." According to this, the joke in the trade is that everyone will retire in 1999. We'll see. . . .

This problem will not, of course, arise in 2099. By then, computers will be able to take care of themselves (as well as H. Sap., if he/she is still around).

I have not invented the unusually large mollusc in Chapter 12. Details (with photographs) of this awesome beast will be found in *Arthur C. Clarke's Mysterious World* (Collins, 1980). *Octopus giganteus* was first positively identified by F. G. Wood and Dr. Joseph Gennaro (*Natural History,* March 1971), both of whom I was happy to get on camera for my *Mysterious World* TV series.

The useful hint on octopus allergies (e.g. what to do if you find one in the toilet) comes from Jacques-Yves Cousteau and Philippe Diole's *Octopus and Squid: The Soft Intelligence* (Cassell, 1973).

And here I must put on record something that has mystified me for many years. In this book, Jacques asserts that though his divers have played with octopuses (very well: octopodes) hundreds of times, they have never once been bitten—and have never even heard of such an incident. Well . . . the *only* time I caught one, off the eastern coast of Australia, it bit me! (see *The Coast of Coral*, Harper & Row, 1956.) I am quite unable to explain this total breakdown of the laws of probability.

According to *Omni* magazine, the question described in Chapter 13 was actually set in a high school intelligence test, and only one genius-type pupil spotted that the printed answer was wrong. I still find this amazing; skeptics may profitably spend a few minutes with scissors and cardboard. The even more incredible story of Srinivasa Ramanujan, mentioned *passim* in the same chapter, will be found in G. H. Hardy's small classic, *A Mathematician's Apology*, and more conveniently in Volume 1 of James Newman's *The World of Mathematics*.

For a crash course in offshore oil drilling operations, I must thank my longtime Sri Lankan friend Cuthbert Charles and his colleagues Walter Jackson and Danny Stephens (all with Brown & Root Vickers Ltd.) and Brian Redden (Technical Services Division Manager, Wharton Williams). They prevented me from making (I hope) too many flagrant errors, and they are in no way responsible for my wilder extrapolations of their truly astonishing achievements—already comparable to much that we will be doing in space during the next century. I apologize for awarding their kindness by sabotaging so much of their handiwork.

The full story of 1974's "Operation JENNIFER" has never

been told, and probably never will be. To my surprise, its director turned out to be an old acquaintance, and I am grateful to him for his evasive but not unhelpful replies to my queries. On the whole, I would prefer not to know too much about the events of that distant summer, so that I am not handicapped by mere facts.

While writing this novel, I was amused to encounter another work of fiction using the *Glomar Explorer,* though (luckily!) for a very different purpose: *Ship of Gold,* by Thomas Allen and Norman Polmar (Macmillan, 1987).

My thanks also to sundry CIA and KGB acquaintances, who would prefer to remain anonymous.

One informant I am happy to identify is Professor William Orr, Dept. of Geological Science, University of Oregon, my erstwhile shipmate on the floating campus SS *Universe*. The plans and documentation he provided on *Glomar Explorer* (now languishing in Suisun Bay, California, between Vallejo and Martinez—you can see her from Highway 680) were essential inputs.

The discovery of major explosive events on the seabed, referred to in Chapter 33, was reported by David B. Prior, Earl H. Doyle, and Michael J. Kaluza in *Science*, vol. 243, pp. 517–9, 27 January 1989, under the title "Evidence for Sediment Eruption on Deep Sea Floor, Gulf of Mexico."

On the very day I was making the final corrections to this manuscript, I learned that there is now strong evidence that oil drilling *can* cause earthquakes. The October 28, 1989, *Science News* cites a paper by Paul Segall of the U.S. Geological Survey, making this claim in the October 1989 issue of *Geology*.

The report on the Neolithic grave quoted in Chapter 34 will be found in *Nature, 276,* 608, 1978.

Ralph C. Merkle's truly mind-boggling paper "Molecular Repair of the Brain" first appeared in the October 1989 issue of

Cryonics (published by ALCOR, 12327, Doherty St., River-side, CA, 92503) to whom I am grateful for an advance copy.

My thanks to Kumar Chitty for information on the U.N. Law of the Sea Convention, directed for many years by the late Ambassador Shirley Hamilton Amarasinghe. It is a great trag-edy that Shirley (the hospitality of whose Park Avenue apart-ment I often enjoyed in the '70s) did not see the culmination of his efforts. He was a wonderful persuader, and had he lived might even have prevented the U.S. and U.K. delegations from shooting themselves in the foot.

I am particularly grateful to my collaborator Gentry Lee (*Cradle,* the *Rama* trilogy) for arranging his schedule so that I could concentrate all my energies on the latest of my 'last' novels. . . .

Very special thanks to Navam and Sally Tambayah—not to mention Tasha and Cindy—for hospitality, WORDSTAR, and faxes. . . .

And, finally: a tribute to my dear friend the late Reginald Ross, who besides many other kindnesses introduced me to Rachmaninoff and Elgar half a century ago, and who died at the age of 91 while this book was being written.

MANDELMEMO

The literature on the Mandelbrot Set, first introduced to the non-IBM world in A. K. Dewdney's "Computer Recreations" (*Scientific American,* Aug. 1985, 16–25), is now enormous. The master's own book, *The Fractal Geometry of Nature* (W. H. Freeman, 1982), is highly technical, and much is inaccessible even to those with delusions of mathematical ability. Neverthe-less, a good deal of the text is informative and witty, so it is well worth skimming. However, it contains only the briefest references to the M-Set, the exploration of which was barely beginning in 1982.

The Beauty of Fractals (H-O. Peitgen and P.H. Richter, Springer-Verlag, 1986) was the first book to show the M-Set in glorious Technicolor, and contains a fascinating (and often amusing) essay by Dr. M. himself on its origins and discovery (invention?). He describes later developments in *The Science of Fractal Images* (edited by H-O. Peitgen and Dietmar Saupe, Springer-Verlag, 1988). Both these books are highly technical.

Much more accessible to the general—though determined—reader is A. K. Dewdney's *The Armchair Universe* (W. H. Freeman, 1988). This contains the original 1985 *Scientific American* article, with updates and information on software available for personal computers. I have been very happy with MandFXP, from Cygnus Software (1215 Davie St., P.O. Box 363, Vancouver BC, V6E 1N4, Canada), and have used this extensively on my AMIGA 2000. While making a TV documentary, "God, the Universe, and Everything Else" for U.K.'s Channel 4, I had the rare privilege of showing Stephen Hawking some beautiful "black holes" I had discovered, while expanding the set until it would have filled the orbit of Mars. Another supplier of M-Set software (for MAC and IBM) is Sintar Software (1001 4th Ave., Suite 3200, Seattle, WA 98154).

Needless to say, there are Mandelbrot "fan magazines," containing hints on speeding up programs, notes from explorers in far-off regions of the set—and even samples of a new literary genre, Fractalfiction. The newsletter of the field is *Amygdala*, edited by Rollo Silver, who also supplies software (Box 111, San Cristobal, NM 87564).

Undoubtedly the best way of appreciating the set is through the videotapes that have been made of it, usually with accompanying music. Most celebrated is "Nothing But Zooms" from Art Matrix (P.O. Box 880, Ithaca, NY 14851). I have also enjoyed "A Fractal Ballet" (The Fractal Stuff Company, P.O. Box 5202, Spokane, WA 99205–5202).

Strictly speaking, the "Utter West" of the M-Set is at exactly -2, not -1.999 . . . to infinity, as stated in Chapter 18. Anyone care to split the difference?

I do not know if there have been any cases of Mandelmania in real life, but I expect to receive reports as soon as this book appears—and waive all responsibility in advance.

APPENDIX

THE COLORS OF INFINITY

IN NOVEMBER 1989, when receiving the Association of Space Explorers Special Achievement Award in Riyadh, Saudi Arabia, I had the privilege of addressing the largest gathering of astronauts and cosmonauts ever assembled at one place. (More than fifty, including Apollo 11's Buzz Aldrin and Mike Collins, and the first "space walker" Alexei Leonov, who is no longer embarrassed at sharing the dedication of *2010: Odyssey Two* with Andrei Sakharov.) I decided to expand their horizons by introducing them to something *really* large, and, with astronaut Prince Sultan bin Salman bin Abdul Aziz in the chair, delivered a lavishly illustrated lecture "The Colors of Infinity: Exploring the Fractal Universe."

The material that follows is extracted from my speech; another portion appears at the beginning of Chapter 15. I'm only sorry that I cannot illustrate it with the gorgeous 35-millimeter slides—and videos—I used at Riyadh.

Today, everybody is familiar with graphs—especially the one with time along the horizontal axis, and the cost of living climbing steadily up the vertical one. The idea that any point on a plane can be expressed by two numbers, usually written *x* and *y*, now appears so obvious that it seems quite surprising that the world of mathematics had to wait until 1637 for Descartes to invent it.

We are still discovering the consequences of that apparently simple idea, and the most amazing is now just ten years old. It's called the Mandelbrot Set (from now on, the M-Set) and you're soon going to meet it everywhere—in the design of fabrics, wallpaper, jewelry, and linoleum. And, I'm afraid, it will be popping out of your TV screen in every other commercial.

Yet the most astonishing feature of the M-Set is its basic *simplicity*. Unlike almost everything else in modern mathematics, any schoolchild can understand how it is produced. Its generation involves nothing more advanced than addition and multiplication; there's no need for such complexities as subtraction and—heaven forbid!—division, let alone any of the more exotic beasts from the mathematical menagerie.

There can be few people in the civilized world who have not encountered Einstein's famous $E = mc^2$, or who would consider it too hopelessly complicated to understand. Well, the equation that defines the M-Set contains the same number of terms, and indeed looks very similar. Here it is:

$$Z = z^2 + c$$

Not very terrifying, is it? Yet the lifetime of the Universe would not be long enough to explore all its ramifications.

The *z*'s and the *c* in Mandelbrot's equation are all *numbers*, not (as in Einstein's) physical quantities like mass and energy. They are the coordinates which specify the position of a point, and the equation controls the way in which it moves, to trace out a pattern.

There's a very simple analog familiar to everyone—those children's books with blank pages sprinkled with numbers, which when joined up in the right order reveal hidden—and often surprising—pictures. The image on a TV screen is produced by a sophisticated application of the same principle.

In theory, anyone who can add and multiply could plot out the M-Set with pen or pencil on a sheet of squared paper. However, as we'll see later, there are certain practical difficulties—notably the fact that a human life span is seldom more than a hundred years. So the set is invariably computer-generated, and usually shown on a visual display unit.

Now, there are two ways of locating a point in space. The more common employs some kind of grid reference—west-east, north-south, or on squared graph paper, a horizontal X-axis and a vertical Y-axis. But there's also the system used in radar, now familiar to most people thanks to countless movies. Here the position of an object is given by (1) its distance from the origin, and (2) its direction, or compass bearing. Incidentally, this is the *natural* system—the one you use automatically and unconsciously when you play any ball game. Then you're concerned with distances and angles, with yourself as the origin.

So think of a computer's VDU as a radar screen, with a single blip on it, whose movements are going to trace out the M-Set. However, before we switch on our radar, I want to make the equation even simpler, to:

$$Z = z^2$$

I've thrown c away, for the moment, and left only the z's. Now let me define them more precisely.

Small z is the initial range of the blip—the distance at which it starts. Big Z is its final distance from the origin. Thus if it was initially 2 units away, by obeying this equation it would promptly hop to a distance of 4.

Nothing to get very excited about, but now comes the modification that makes all the difference:

$$Z \rightleftharpoons z^2$$

That double arrow is a two-way traffic sign, indicating that the numbers flow in both directions. This time, we don't stop at $Z = 4$; we make *that* equal to a new z—which promptly gives us a second Z of 16, and so on. In no time we've generated the series

$$256, \qquad 65536, \qquad 4294967296 \ldots$$

and the spot that started only 2 units from the center is heading toward infinity in giant steps of ever-increasing magnitude.

This process of going around and around a loop is called "iteration." It's like a dog chasing its own tail, except that a dog doesn't get anywhere. But mathematical iteration can take us to some very strange places indeed—as we shall soon discover.

Now we're ready to turn on our radar. Most displays have range circles at 10, 20 . . . 100 kilometers from the center. We will require only a single circle, at a range of 1. There's no need to specify any units, as we're dealing with pure numbers. Make them centimeters or light-years, as you please.

Let's suppose that the initial position of our blip is anywhere on this circle—the bearing doesn't matter. So z is 1.

And because 1 squared is still 1, so is Z. And it remains at that value, because no matter how many times you square 1, it always remains exactly 1. The blip may hop around and around the circle, *but it always stays on it.*

Now consider the case where the initial z is greater than 1.

We've already seen how rapidly the blip shoots off to infinity if z equals 2—but the same thing will happen sooner or later, even if it's only a microscopic shade more than 1—say 1.000000000000000000001. Watch:

At the first squaring, Z becomes

1.000000000000000000002

then

1.000000000000000000004
1.000000000000000000008
1.000000000000000000016
1.000000000000000000032

and so on for pages of printout. For all practical purposes, the value is still exactly 1. The blip hasn't moved visibly outward or inward; it's still on the circle at range 1.

But those zeros are slowly being whittled away, as the digits march inexorably across from the right. Quite suddenly, something appears in the third, second, first decimal place—and the numbers explode after a very few additional terms, as this example shows:

| 1.001 | 1.002 | 1.004 | 1.008 | 1.016 | 1.032 |
| 1.066 | 1.136 | 1.292 | 1.668 | 2.783 | 7.745 |

| 59.987 | 3598.467 | 12948970 |

167675700000000

281151400000000000000000000000
(Overflow)

There could be a million—a billion—zeros on the right-hand side, and the result would still be the same. Eventually the digits would creep up to the decimal point—and then Z would take off to infinity.

Now let's look at the other case. Suppose z is a microscopic amount *less* than 1—say something like

$$.99999999999999999999$$

As before, nothing much happens for a long time as we go around the loop, except that the numbers on the far right get steadily smaller. But after a few thousand or million iterations— catastrophe! Z suddenly shrinks to nothing, dissolving in an endless string of zeros. . . .

Check it out on your computer. It can only handle twelve digits? Well, no matter how many you had to play with, you'd still get the same answer. Trust me. . . .

The results of this "program" can be summarized in three laws that may seem too trivial to be worth formulating. But no mathematical truth is trivial, and in a few more steps these laws will take us into a universe of mind-boggling wonder and beauty.

Here are the three laws of the "Squaring" Program:

1. If the input z is exactly *equal* to 1, the output Z always remains 1.
2. If the input is *more than* 1, the output eventually becomes infinite.
3. If the input is *less than* 1, the output eventually becomes zero.

That circle of radius 1 is therefore a kind of map—or, if you like, fence—dividing the plane into two distinct territories. Outside it, numbers which obey the squaring law have the freedom of infinity; numbers inside it are prisoners, trapped and doomed to ultimate extinction.

At this point, someone may say: "You've only talked about *ranges*—distances from the origin. To fix the blip's position, you have to give its bearing as well. What about that?"

Very true. Fortunately, in this selection process—this division of the z's into two distinct classes—bearings are irrelevant; the same thing happens whichever direction *r* is pointing. For this simple example—let's call it the S-set—we can ignore them. When we come on to the more complicated case of the M-Set, where the bearing *is* important, there's a very neat mathematical trick which takes care of it, by using complex or imaginary numbers (which really aren't at all complex, still less imaginary). But we don't need them here, and I promise not to mention them again.

The S-set lies inside a *map,* and its frontier is the circle enclosing it. That circle is simply a continuous line with no thickness. If you could examine it with a microscope of infinite power, it would always look exactly the same. You could expand the S-set to the size of the Universe; its boundary would still be a line of zero thickness. Yet there are no holes in it; it's an absolutely impenetrable barrier, forever separating the z's less than one from those greater than one.

Now, at last, we're ready to tackle the M-Set, where these commonsense ideas are turned upside down. Fasten your seat belts.

During the 1970s, the French mathematician Benoit Mandelbrot, working at Harvard and IBM, started to investigate the equation which has made him famous, and which I will now write in the dynamic form:

$$Z \rightleftharpoons z^2 + c$$

The only difference between this and the equation we have used to describe the S-set is the term *c.* This—not z—is now the starting point of our mapping operation. The first time around the loop, z is put equal to zero.

It seems a trifling change, and no one could have imagined the universe it would reveal. Mandelbrot himself did not obtain the first crude glimpses until the spring of 1980, when vague patterns started to emerge on computer printouts. He had begun to peer through Keats'

> Charm'd magic casements, opening on the foam
> Of perilous seas, in faery lands forlorn . . .

As we shall learn later, that word "foam" is surprisingly appropriate.

The new equation asks and answers the same question as the earlier one: What shape is the "territory" mapped out when we put numbers into it? For the S-set it was a circle with radius 1. Let's see what happens when we start with this value in the M-equation. You should be able to do it in your head—for the first few steps. After a few dozen, even a supercomputer may blow a gasket.

For starters, $z = 0$, $c = 1$. So $Z = 1$

First loop: $Z = 1^2 + 1 = 2$

Second loop: $Z = 2^2 + 1 = 5$

Third loop: $Z = 5^2 + 1 = 26$

Fourth loop: $Z = 26^2 + 1$ . . . and so on.

I once set my computer to work out the higher terms (about the limit of my programming ability) and it produced only two more values before it had to start approximating:

$$1, 2, 5, 26, 677, 458330,$$
$$21006640000$$
$$441278900000000000000000$$

At that point it gave up, because it doesn't believe there are any numbers with more than 38 digits.

However, even the first two or three terms are quite enough to show that the M-Set must have a very different shape from the perfectly circular S-set. A point at distance 1 is in the S-set; indeed, it defines its boundary. A point at that same distance may be outside the boundary of the M-Set.

Note that I say "may," not "must." It all depends on the initial *direction*, or bearing, of the starting point, which we have been able to ignore hitherto because it did not affect our discussion of the (perfectly symmetrical) S-set. As it turns out, the M-Set is only symmetrical about the X, or horizontal, axis.

One might have guessed that, from the nature of the equation. But no one could possibly have intuited its real appearance. If the question had been put to me in virginal pre-Mandelbrot days, I would probably have hazarded: "Something like an ellipse, squashed along the Y-axis." I might even (though I doubt it) have correctly guessed that it would be shifted toward the left, or minus, direction.

At this point, I would like to try a thought experiment on you. The M-Set being literally indescribable, here's my attempt to describe it:

Imagine you're looking straight down on a rather plump turtle, swimming westward. It's been crossed with a swordfish, so has a narrow spike pointing ahead of it. Its entire perimeter is festooned with bizarre marine growths—and with baby turtles of assorted sizes, which have smaller weeds growing on them. . . .

I defy you to find a description like *that* in any math textbook. And if you think you can do better when you've seen the real beast, you're welcome to try. (I suspect that the insect world might provide better analogies; there may even be a

Mandelbeetle lurking in the Brazilian rain forests. Too bad we'll never know.)

Here is the first crude approximation, shorn of details— much like Conroy Castle's "Lake Mandelbrot" (Chapter 18). If you like to fill its blank spaces with the medieval cartographers' favorite "Here be dragons" you will hardly be exaggerating.

First of all, note that—as I've already remarked—it's shifted to the left (or west, if you prefer) of the S-set, which of course extends from +1 to -1 along the X-axis. The M-Set only gets to 0.25 on the right along the axis, though above and below the axis it bulges out to just beyond 0.4.

On the left-hand side, the map stretches to about -1.4, and then it sprouts a peculiar spike—or antenna—which reaches out to exactly -2.0. As far as the M-Set is concerned, there is *nothing* beyond this point; it is the edge of the Universe. Mandelbrot

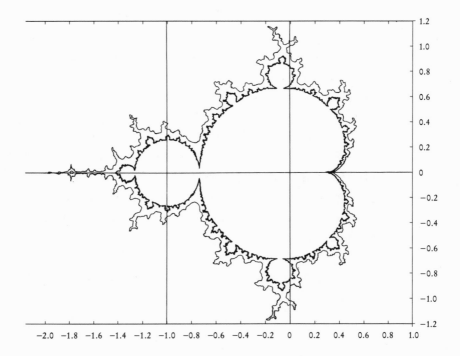

fans call it the "Utter West," and you might like to see what happens when you make c equal to -2. Z doesn't converge to zero—but it doesn't escape to infinity either, so the point belongs to the set—*just.* But if you make c the slightest bit larger, say -2.00000 . . . 000001, before you know it you're passing Pluto and heading for Quasar West.

Now we come to the most important distinction between the two sets. The S-set has a nice, clean line for its boundary. The frontier of the M-Set is, to say the least, fuzzy. Just how fuzzy you will begin to understand when we start to "zoom" into it; only then will we see the incredible flora and fauna which flourish in that disputed territory.

The boundary—if one can call it that—of the M-Set is not a simple line; it is something which Euclid never imagined, and for which there is no word in ordinary language. Mandelbrot, whose command of English (and American) is awesome, has ransacked the dictionary for suggestive nouns. A few examples: foams, sponges, dusts, webs, nets, curds. He himself coined the technical name *fractal,* and is now putting up a spirited rear-guard action to stop anyone from defining it too precisely.

Computers can easily make "snapshots" of the M-Set at any magnification, and even in black and white they are fascinating. However, by a simple trick they can be colored, and transformed into objects of amazing, even surreal, beauty.

The original equation, of course, is no more concerned with color than is Euclid's *Elements of Geometry.* But if we instruct the computer to color any given region in accordance with the number of times z goes around the loop before it decides *whether or not* it belongs to the M-Set, the results are gorgeous.

Thus the colors, though arbitrary, are not meaningless. An exact analogy is found in cartography. Think of the contour lines on a relief map, which show elevations above sea level. The spaces between them are often colored so that the eye can more easily grasp the information conveyed. Ditto with bathymetric charts; the deeper the ocean, the darker the blue. The mapmaker can make the colors anything he likes, and is guided by aesthetics as much as geography.

It's just the same here—except that *these* contour lines are set automatically by the speed of the calculation—I won't go into details. I have not discovered what genius first had this idea—perhaps Monsieur M. himself—but it turns them into fantastic works of art. And you should see them when they're animated. . . .

One of the many strange thoughts that the M-Set generates is this. In principle, it could have been discovered as soon as the human race learned to count. In practice, since even a "low magnification" image may involve *billions* of calculations, there was no way in which it could even be glimpsed before computers were invented! And such movies as Art Matrix' *Nothing But Zooms* would have required the entire present world population to calculate night and day for years—without making a *single* mistake in multiplying together trillions of hundred-digit numbers. . . .

I began by saying that the Mandelbrot Set is the most extraordinary discovery in the history of mathematics. For who could have possibly imagined that so absurdly simple an equation could have generated such—literally—infinite complexity, and such unearthly beauty?

The Mandelbrot Set is, as I have tried to explain, essentially a map. We've all read those stories about maps which reveal the location of hidden treasure.

Well, in this case—the map *is* the treasure!

Colombo, Sri Lanka: 1990 February 28